CONTEMPORARY AMERIC___ ___ION

DESCENT OF MAN

T. Coraghessan Boyle is the author of a collection of
short stories, *Greasy Lake* (Penguin, 1986), and two
novels, *Water Music* and *Budding Prospects* (both
available from Penguin). His stories appear regu-
larly in *Esquire*, *The Paris Review*, *The Atlantic*,
and elsewhere. He is currently at work on a new
novel about the intertwined destinies of three fami-
lies during three hundred years of Hudson Valley
history. Mr. Boyle lives in Los Angeles.

DESCENT OF
MAN

STORIES BY

T. Coraghessan Boyle

PENGUIN BOOKS

PENGUIN BOOKS
Published by the Penguin Group
Viking Penguin Inc., 40 West 23rd Street, New York 10010, U.S.A.
Penguin Books Ltd, 27 Wrights Lane, London W8 5TZ, England
Penguin Books Australia Ltd, Ringwood, Victoria, Australia
Penguin Books Canada Ltd, 2801 John Street,
Markham, Ontario, Canada L3R 1B4
Penguin Books (N.Z.) Ltd, 182–190 Wairau Road,
Auckland 10, New Zealand

Penguin Books Ltd, Registered Offices:
Harmondsworth, Middlesex, England

First published in the United States of America by
Atlantic Monthly Press, Little, Brown and Company, 1979
Published in Penguin Books 1987

3 5 7 9 10 8 6 4 2

LIBRARY OF CONGRESS CATALOGING IN PUBLICATION DATA
Boyle, T. Coraghessan.
Descent of man.
(Contemporary American fiction)
I. Title.   II. Series.
[PS3552.0932D4 1986]   813'.54   86-15131
ISBN 0 14 00.9286 2

"Descent of Man" and "The Second Swimming" first appeared in the *Paris Review;*
"The Champ" and "John Barleycorn Lives" in the *Atlantic Monthly;* "We Are
Norsemen" in *Harper's;* "Heart of a Champion" in *Esquire;* "Bloodfall" in *Epoch;*
"A Women's Restaurant" in *Penthouse;* "Caye" in *Tri-Quarterly;* "Green Hell" in the
Transatlantic Review; "Earth, Moon" in *Fiction;* "De Rerum Natura" in *Quest/77;*
"Quetzalcóatl Lite" in *Quest/78;* "Drowning" in the *South Dakota Review.*
Some of "The Extinction Tales" was suggested by material in Jay Williams's
Fall of the Sparrow (Oxford, 1951).

Printed in the United States of America by
R. R. Donnelley & Sons Company, Harrisonburg, Virginia
Set in Caledonia

For T. Senior and Rosemary,
and especially
for you,
K.K.

I could never have achieved what I have done had I been stubbornly set on clinging to my origins. . . . In fact, to give up being stubborn was the supreme commandment I laid upon myself; free ape as I was, I submitted myself to that yoke.

—Franz Kafka, "A Report to an Academy"

Ungowa!

—Johnny Weismuller, *Tarzan Finds a Son*

Contents

DESCENT OF MAN

Descent of Man

I WAS LIVING WITH A WOMAN who suddenly began to stink. It was very difficult. The first time I confronted her she merely smiled. "Occupational hazard," she said. The next time she curled her lip. There were other problems too. Hairs, for instance. Hairs that began to appear on her clothing, sharp and black and brutal. Invariably I would awake to find these hairs in my mouth, or I would glance into the mirror to see them slashing like razor edges across the collars of my white shirts. Then too there was the fruit. I began to discover moldering bits of it about the house—apple and banana most characteristically—but plum and tangelo or even passion fruit and yim-yim were not at all anomalous. These fruit fragments occurred principally in the bedroom, on the pillow, surrounded by darkening spots. It was not long before I located their source: they lay hidden like gems in the long wild hanks of her hair. Another occupational hazard.

Jane was in the habit of sitting before the air conditioner when she came home from work, fingering out her hair, drying the sweat from her face and neck in the cool hum of the machine, fruit bits sifting silently to the carpet, black hairs drifting like feathers. On these occasions the room would fill with the stink of her, bestial and fetid. And I would find my eyes watering, my mind imaging the dark rotting trunks of the rain forest, stained sienna and mandalay and Hooker's green with the excrements dropped from above. My ears would keen with the whistling and crawking of the jungle birds, the screechings of the snot-nosed apes in the branches. And then, slack-faced and tight-boweled, I would step into the bathroom and retch, the sweetness of my own intestinal secrets a balm against the potent hairy stench of her.

One evening, just after her bath (the faintest odor lingered, yet still it was so trenchant I had to fight the impulse to get up and urinate on a tree or a post or something), I laid my hand casually across her belly and was suddenly startled to see an insect flit from its cover, skate up the swell of her abdomen, and bury itself in her navel. "Good Christ," I said.

"Hm?" she returned, peering over the cover of her Yerkish reader.

"That," I said. "That bug, that insect, that vermin."

She sat up, plucked the thing from its cachette, raised it to her lips and popped it between her front teeth. "Louse," she said, sucking. "Went down to the old age home on Thirteenth Street to pick them up."

I anticipated her: "Not for—?"

"Why certainly, potpie—so Konrad can experience a tangible gratification of his social impulses during the grooming ritual. You know: you scratch my back, I scratch yours."

I lay in bed that night sweating, thinking about Jane and those slippery-fingered monkeys poking away at her, and listening for the lice crawling across her scalp or nestling their bloody little siphons in the tufts under her arms. Finally, about four, I got up and took three Doriden. I woke at two in the afternoon, an insect in my ear. It was only an earwig. I had missed my train, failed to call in at the office. There was a note from Jane: Pick me up at four. Konrad sends love.

The Primate Center stood in the midst of a macadamized acre or two, looking very much like a school building: faded brick, fluted columns, high mesh fences. Finger paintings and mobiles hung in the windows, misshapen ceramics crouched along the sills. A flag raggled at the top of a whitewashed flagpole. I found myself bending to examine the cornerstone: Asa Priff Grammar School, 1939. Inside it was dark and cool, the halls were lined with lockers and curling watercolors, the linoleum gleamed like a shy smile. I stepped into the BOYS' ROOM. The urinals were a foot and a half from the floor. Designed for little people, I mused. Youngsters. Hardly big enough to hold their little peters without the teacher's help. I smiled, and situated myself over one of the toy urinals, the strong honest scent of Pine-Sol in my nostrils. At that moment the door wheezed open and a chimpanzee shuffled in. He was dressed in shorts, shirt and bow tie. He nodded to me, it seemed, and made a few odd gestures with his hands as he moved up to the urinal beside mine. Then he opened his fly and pulled out an enormous slick red organ like a peeled banana. I looked away, embarrassed, but could hear him urinating mightily. The stream hissed against the porcelain like a thunderstorm, rattled the drain as it went down. My own water wouldn't come. I began to feel foolish. The chimp shook himself daintily, zippered up, pulled the plunger, crossed to the sink, washed and dried his hands, and left. I found I no longer had to go.

Out in the hallway the janitor was leaning on his flathead

broom. The chimp stood before him gesticulating with manic dexterity: brushing his forehead and tugging his chin, slapping his hands under his armpits, tapping his wrists, his tongue, his ear, his lip. The janitor watched intently. Suddenly—after a particularly virulent flurry—the man burst into laughter, rich braying globes of it. The chimp folded his lip and joined in, adding his weird nasal snickering to the janitor's barrel-laugh. I stood by the door to the BOYS' ROOM in a quandary. I began to feel that it might be wiser to wait in the car—but then I didn't want to call attention to myself, darting in and out like that. The janitor might think I was stealing paper towels or something. So I stood there, thinking to have a word with him after the chimp moved on—with the expectation that he could give me some grassroots insight into the nature of Jane's job. But the chimp didn't move on. The two continued laughing, now harder than ever. The janitor's face was tear-streaked. Each time he looked up the chimp produced a gesticular flurry that would stagger him again. Finally the janitor wound down a bit, and still chuckling, held out his hands, palms up. The chimp flung his arms up over his head and then heaved them down again, rhythmically slapping the big palms with his own. "Right on! Mastuh Konrad," the janitor said, "Right on!" The chimp grinned, then hitched up his shorts and sauntered off down the hall. The janitor turned back to his broom, still chuckling.

I cleared my throat. The broom began a geometrically precise course up the hall toward me. It stopped at my toes, the ridge of detritus flush with the pinions of my wingtips. The janitor looked up. The pupil of his right eye was fixed in the corner, beneath the lid, and the white was red. There was an ironic gap between his front teeth. "Kin ah do sumfin fo yo, mah good man?" he said.

"I'm waiting for Miss Good."

"Ohhh, Miz *Good*," he said, nodding his head. "Fust ah

tought yo was thievin paypuh tow-els outen de Boys' Room
but den when ah sees yo standin dere rigid as de Venus de
Milo ah thinks to mahsef: he is some kinda new sculpture de
stoodents done made is what he is." He was squinting up at
me and grinning like we'd just come back from sailing around
the world together.

"That's a nice broom," I said.

He looked at me steadily, grinning still. "Yo's wonderin
what me and Mastuh Konrad was jivin bout up dere, isn't yo?
Well, ah tells yo: he was relatin a hoomerous anecdote, de
punch line ob which has deep cosmic implications in dat it
establishes a common groun between monks and Ho-mo sa-
piens despite dere divergent ancestries." He shook his head,
chortled. "Yes in-deed, dat Mastuh Konrad is quite de wit."

"You mean to tell me you actually understand all that lip-
pulling and finger-waving?" I was beginning to feel a nameless
sense of outrage.

"Oh sartinly, mah good man. Dat ASL."

"What?"

"ASL is what we was talkin. A-merican Sign Language.
De-veloped for de deef n dumb. Yo sees, Mastuh Konrad is
sumfin ob a genius round here. He can commoonicate de mos
esoteric i-deas in bof ASL and Yerkish, re-spond to and translate English, French, German and Chinese. Fack, it was Miz
Good was tellin me dat Konrad is workin right now on a
Yerkish translation ob Darwin's *De-scent o Man*. He is mainly
into anthro-pology, yo knows, but he has cultivated a in-ter-
ess in udder fields too. Dis lass fall he done undertook a
Yerkish translation ob Chomsky's *Language and Mind* and
Nietzsche's *Jenseits von Gut und Böse*. And dat's some pretty
heavy shit, Jackson."

I was hot with outrage. "Stuff," I said. "Stuff and non-
sense."

"No sense in feelin personally treatened by Mastuh Konrad's chievements, mah good fellow—yo's got to ree-lize dat he is a genius."

A word came to me: "Bullhonk," I said. And turned to leave.

The janitor caught me by the shirtsleeve. "He is now scorin his turd opera," he whispered. I tore away from him and stamped out of the building.

Jane was waiting in the car. I climbed in, cranked down the sunroof and opened the air vents.

At home I poured a water glass of gin, held it to my nostrils and inhaled. Jane sat before the air conditioner, her hair like a urinal mop, stinking. Black hairs cut the atmosphere, fruit bits whispered to the carpet. Occasionally the tip of my tongue entered the gin. I sniffed and tasted, thinking of plastic factories and turpentine distilleries and rich sulfurous smoke. On my way to the bedroom I poured a second glass.

In the bedroom I sniffed gin and dressed for dinner. "Jane?" I called, "shouldn't you be getting ready?" She appeared in the doorway. She was dressed in her work clothes: jeans and sweatshirt. The sweatshirt was gray and hooded. There were yellow stains on the sleeves. I thought of the lower depths of animal cages, beneath the floor meshing. "I figured I'd go like this," she said. I was knotting my tie. "And I wish you'd stop insisting on baths every night—I'm getting tired of smelling like a coupon in a detergent box. It's unnatural. Unhealthy."

In the car on the way to the restaurant I lit a cigar, a cheap twisted black thing like half a pepperoni. Jane sat hunched against her door, unwashed. I had never before smoked a cigar. I tried to start a conversation but Jane said she didn't feel like talking: talk seemed so useless, such an anachronism. We drove on in silence. And I reflected that this was not the

Jane I knew and loved. Where, I wondered, was the girl who changed wigs three or four times a day and sported nails like a Chinese emperor?—and where was the girl who dressed like an Arabian bazaar and smelled like the trade winds?

She was committed. The project, the study, grants. I could read the signs: she was growing away from me.

The restaurant was dark, a maze of rocky gardens, pancake-leafed vegetation, black fountains. We stood squinting just inside the door. Birds whistled, carp hissed through the pools. Somewhere a monkey screeched. Jane put her hand on my shoulder and whispered in my ear. "Siamang," she said. At that moment the leaves parted beside us: a rubbery little fellow emerged and motioned us to sit on a bench beneath a wicker birdcage. He was wearing a soiled loincloth and eight or ten necklaces of yellowed teeth. His hair flamed out like a brushfire. In the dim light from the braziers I noticed his nostrils—both shrunken and pinched, as if once pierced straight through. His face was of course inscrutable. As soon as we were seated he removed my socks and shoes, Jane's sneakers, and wrapped our feet in what I later learned were plantain leaves. I started to object—I bitterly resent anyone looking at my feet—but Jane shushed me. We had waited three months for reservations.

The maitre d' signed for us to follow, and led us through a dripping stone-walled tunnel to an outdoor garden where the flagstones gave way to dirt and we found ourselves on a narrow plant-choked path. He licked along like an iguana and we hurried to keep up. Wet fronds slapped back in my face, creepers snatched at my ankles, mud sucked at the plantain leaves on my feet. The scents of mold and damp and long-lying urine hung in the air, and I thought of the men's room at the subway station. It was dark as a womb. I offered Jane my hand, but she refused it. Her breathing was fast. The monkey chatter was loud as a zoo afire. "Far out," she said. I slapped a mosquito on my neck.

A moment later we found ourselves seated at a bamboo table overhung with branch and vine. Across from us sat Dr. and Mrs. U-Hwak-Lo, director of the Primate Center and wife. A candle guttered between them. I cleared my throat, and then began idly tracing my finger around the circular hole cut in the table's center. The Doctor's ears were the size of peanuts. "Glad you two could make it," he said. "I've long been urging Jane to sample some of our humble island fare." I smiled, crushed a spider against the back of my chair. The Doctor's English was perfect, pure Martha's Vineyard—he sounded like Ted Kennedy's insurance salesman. His wife's was weak: "Yes," she said, "nussing cook here, all roar." "How exciting!" said Jane. And then the conversation turned to primates, and the Center.

Mrs. U-Hwak-Lo and I smiled at one another. Jane and the Doctor were already deeply absorbed in a dialogue concerning the incidence of anal retention in chimps deprived of Frisbee coordination during the sensorimotor period. I gestured toward them with my head and arched my eyebrows wittily. Mrs. U-Hwak-Lo giggled. It was then that Jane's proximity began to affect me. The close wet air seemed to concentrate her essence, distill its potency. The U-Hwak-Los seemed unaffected. I began to feel queasy. I reached for the fingerbowl and drank down its contents. Mrs. U-Hwak-Lo smiled. It was coconut oil. Just then the waiter appeared carrying a wooden bowl the size of a truck tire. A single string of teeth slapped against his breastbone as he set the bowl down and slipped off into the shadows. The Doctor and Jane were oblivious—they were talking excitedly, occasionally lapsing into what I took to be ASL, ear- and nose- and lip-picking like a manager and his third-base coach. I peered into the bowl: it was filled to the rim with clean-picked chicken bones. Mrs. U-Hwak-Lo nodded, grinning: "No on-tray," she said. "Appeticer." At that moment a simian screamed somewhere close, screamed like death itself. Jane looked up. "Rhesus," she said.

On my return from the men's room I had some difficulty locating the table in the dark. I had already waded through two murky fountains and was preparing to plunge through my third when I heard Mrs. U-Hwak-Lo's voice behind me. "Here," she said. "Make quick, repass now serve." She took my hand and led me back to the table. "Oh, they're enormously resourceful," the Doctor was saying as I stumbled into my chair, pants wet to the knees. "They first employ a general anesthetic—a distillation of the chu-bok root—and then the chef (who logically doubles as village surgeon) makes a circular incision about the macaque's cranium, carefully peeling back the already-shaven scalp, and stanching the blood flow quite effectively with maura-ro, a highly absorbent powder derived from the tamana leaf. He then removes both the frontal and parietal plates to expose the brain . . ." I looked at Jane: she was rapt. I wasn't really listening. My attention was directed toward what I took to be the main course, which had appeared in my absence. An unsteady pinkish mound now occupied the center of the table, completely obscuring the circular hole—it looked like cherry vanilla yogurt, a carton and a half, perhaps two. On closer inspection I noticed several black hairs peeping out from around its flaccid edges. And thought immediately of the bush-headed maitre d'. I pointed to one of the hairs, remarking to Mrs. U-Hwak-Lo that the rudiments of culinary hygiene could be a little more rigorously observed among the staff. She smiled. Encouraged, I asked her what exactly the dish was. "Much delicacy," she

said. "Very rare find in land of Lincoln." At that moment the
waiter appeared and handed each of us a bamboo stick beaten
flat and sharpened at one end.

". . . then the tribal elders or visiting dignitaries are seated
around the table," the Doctor was saying. "The chef has pre-
viously of course located the macaque beneath the table, the
exposed part of the creature's brain protruding from the hole
in its center. After the feast, the lower ranks of the village
population divide up the remnants. It's really quite efficient."

"How fascinating!" said Jane. "Shall we try some?"

"By all means . . . but tell me, how has Konrad been coming with that Yerkish epic he's been working up?"

Jane turned to answer, bamboo stick poised: "Oh I'm so
glad you asked—I'd almost forgotten. He's finished his tenth
book and tells me he'll be doing two more—out of deference
to the Miltonic tradition. Isn't that a groove?"

"Yes," said the Doctor, gesturing toward the rosy lump in
the center of the table. "Yes it is. He's certainly—and I hope
you won't mind the pun—a brainy fellow. Ho-ho."

"Oh Doctor," Jane laughed, and plunged her stick into the
pink. Beneath the table, in the dark, a tiny fist clutched at my
pantleg.

I missed work again the following day. This time it took five
Doriden to put me under. I had lain in bed sweating and
tossing, listening to Jane's quiet breathing, inhaling her
fumes. At dawn I dozed off, dreamed briefly of elementary
school cafeterias swarming with knickered chimps and wel-
tered with trays of cherry vanilla yogurt, and woke stale-
mouthed. Then I took the pills. It was three-thirty when I
woke again. There was a note from Jane: Bringing Konrad
home for dinner. Vacuum rug and clean toilet.

Konrad was impeccably dressed—long pants, platform
wedgies, cuff links. He smelled of eau de cologne, Jane of used

litter. They arrived during the seven o'clock news. I opened
the door for them. "Hello Jane," I said. We stood at the door,
awkward, silent. "Well?" she said. "Aren't you going to greet
our guest?" "Hello Konrad," I said. And then: "I believe we
met in the boys' room at the Center the other day?" He
bowed deeply, straight-faced, his upper lip like a halved can-
taloupe. Then he broke into a snicker, turned to Jane and
juggled out an impossible series of gestures. Jane laughed.
Something caught in my throat. "Is he trying to say something?" I asked. "Oh potpie," she said, "it was nothing—just a
little quote from Yeats."

"Yeats?"

"Yes, you know: 'An aged man is but a paltry thing.' "

Jane served watercress sandwiches and animal crackers as
hors d'oeuvres. She brought them into the living room on a
cut-glass serving tray and set them down before Konrad and
me, where we sat on the sofa, watching the news. Then she
returned to the kitchen. Konrad plucked up a tiny sandwich
and swallowed it like a communion wafer, sucking the tips of
his fingers. Then he lifted the tray and offered it to me. I
declined. "No thank you," I said. Konrad shrugged, set the
plate down in his lap and carefully stacked all the sandwiches
in its center. I pretended to be absorbed with the news: actually I studied him, half-face. He was filling the gaps in his
sandwich-construction with animal crackers. His lower lip
protruded, his ears were rubbery, he was balding. With both
hands he crushed the heap of crackers and sandwiches together and began kneading it until it took on the consistency
of raw dough. Then he lifted the whole thing to his mouth and
swallowed it without chewing. There were no whites to his
eyes.

Konrad's only reaction to the newscast was a burst of excitement over a war story—the reporter stood against the
wasteland of treadless tanks and recoilless guns in Thailand or

Syria or Chile; huts were burning, old women weeping. "Wow-wow! Eeeeeeee! Er-er-er-er," Konrad said. Jane appeared in the kitchen doorway, hands dripping. "What is it, Konrad?" she said. He made a series of violent gestures. "Well?" I asked. She translated: "Konrad says that 'the pig oppressors' genocidal tactics will lead to their mutual extermination and usher in a new golden age . . .' "—here she hesitated, looked up at him to continue (he was springing up and down on the couch, flailing his fists as though they held whips and scourges)—" '. . . of freedom and equality for all, regardless of race, creed, color—or genus.' I wouldn't worry," she added, "it's just his daily slice of revolutionary rhetoric. He'll calm down in a minute—he likes to play Che, but he's basically nonviolent."

Ten minutes later Jane served dinner. Konrad, with remarkable speed and coordination, consumed four cans of fruit cocktail, thirty-two spareribs, half a dozen each of oranges, apples and pomegranates, two cheeseburgers and three quarts of chocolate malted. In the kitchen, clearing up, I commented to Jane about our guest's prodigious appetite. He was sitting in the other room, listening to *Don Giovanni*, sipping brandy. Jane said that he was a big, active male and that she could attest to his need for so many calories. "How much does he weigh?" I asked. "Stripped," she said, "one eighty-one. When he stands up straight he's four eight and three quarters." I mulled over this information while I scraped away at the dishes, filed them in the dishwasher, neat ranks of blue china. A few moments later I stepped into the living room to observe Jane stroking Konrad's ears, his head in her lap. I stand five seven, one forty-three.

When I returned from work the following day, Jane was gone. Her dresser drawers were bare, the closet empty. There were white rectangles on the wall where her Rousseau reproductions had hung. The top plank of the bookcase was ribbed with the dust-prints of her Edgar Rice Burroughs collection. Her girls' softball trophy, her natural foods cookbook, her oaken cudgel, her moog, her wok: all gone. There were no notes. A pain jabbed at my sternum, tears started in my eyes. I was alone, deserted, friendless. I began to long even for the stink of her. On the pillow in the bedroom I found a fermenting chunk of pineapple. And sobbed.

By the time I thought of the Primate Center the sun was already on the wane. It was dark when I got there. Loose gravel grated beneath my shoes in the parking lot; the flag snapped at the top of its pole; the lights grinned lickerishly from the Center's windows. Inside the lighting was subdued, the building hushed. I began searching through the rooms, opening and slamming doors. The linoleum glowed all the way up the long corridor. At the far end I heard someone whistling "My Old Kentucky Home." It was the janitor. "Howdedo," he said. "Wut kin ah do fo yo at such a inauspicious hour ob de night?"

I was candid with him. "I'm looking for Miss Good."

"Ohhh, she leave bout fo-turdy evy day—sartinly yo should be well apprised ob dat fack."

"I thought she might be working late tonight."

"Noooo, no chance ob dat." He was staring at the floor.

"Mind if I look for myself?"

"Mah good man, ah trusts yo is not intimatin dat ah would dis-kise de troof . . . far be it fum me to pre-varicate jus to proteck a young lady wut run off fum a man dat doan unnerstan her needs nor 'low her to spress de natchrul inclination ob her soul."

At that moment a girlish giggle sounded from down the hall. Jane's girlish giggle. The janitor's right hand spread itself across my chest. "Ah wooden insinooate mahsef in de middle ob a highly sinificant speriment if ah was yo, Jackson," he said, hissing through the gap in his teeth. I pushed by him and started down the corridor. Jane's laugh leaped out again. From the last door on my left. I hurried. Suddenly the Doctor and his wife stepped from the shadows to block the doorway. "Mr. Horne," said the Doctor, arms folded against his chest, "take hold of yourself. We are conducting a series of experiments here that I simply cannot allow you to—"

"A fig for your experiments," I shouted. "I want to speak to my, my—roommate." I could hear the janitor's footsteps behind me. "Get out of my way, Doctor," I said. Mrs. U-Hwak-Lo smiled. I felt panicky. Thought of the Tong Wars. "Is dey a problem here, Doc?" the janitor said, his breath hot on the back of my neck. I broke. Grabbed the Doctor by his elbows, wheeled around and shoved him into the janitor. They went down on the linoleum like spastic skaters. I applied my shoulder to the door and battered my way in, Mrs. U-Hwak-Lo's shrill in my ear: "You make big missake, Misser!" Inside I found Jane, legs and arms bare, pinching a lab smock across her chest. She looked puzzled at first, then annoyed. She stepped up to me, made some rude gestures in my face. I could hear scrambling in the hallway behind me. Then I saw Konrad—in a pair of baggy BVDs. I grabbed Jane. But Konrad was there in an instant—he hit me like the grill of a Cadillac and I spun across the room, tumbling desks and chairs as I went. I slumped against the chalkboard. The door slammed: Jane was gone. Konrad swelled his chest, swayed toward me, the fluorescent lights hissing overhead, the chalkboard cold against the back of my neck. And I looked up into the black eyes, teeth, fur, rock-ribbed arms.

The Champ

ANGELO D. was training hard. This challenger, Kid Gullet, would be no pushover. In fact, the Kid hit him right where he lived: he was worried. He'd been champ for thirty-seven years and all that time his records had stood like Mount Rushmore—and now this Kid was eating them up. Fretful, he pushed his plate away.

"But Angelo, you ain't done already?" His trainer, Spider Decoud, was all over him. "That's what—a piddling hundred and some odd flapjacks and seven quarts a milk?"

"He's on to me, Spider. He found out about the ulcer and now he's going to hit me with enchiladas and shrimp in cocktail sauce."

"Don't fret it, Killer. We'll get him with the starches and heavy syrups. He's just a kid, twenty-two. What does he know about eating? Look, get up and walk it off and we'll do a kidney and kipper course, okay? And then maybe four or five

dozen poached eggs. C'mon, Champ, lift that fork. You want
to hold onto the title or not?"

First it was pickled eggs. Eighty-three pickled eggs in an
hour and a half. The record had stood since 1941. They said it
was like DiMaggio's consecutive-game hitting streak: unap-
proachable. A world apart. But then, just three months ago,
Angelo had picked up the morning paper and found himself
unforked: a man who went by the name of Kid Gullet had put
down 108 of them. In the following weeks Angelo had seen his
records toppled like a string of dominoes: gherkins, pullets,
persimmons, oysters, pretzels, peanuts, scalloped potatoes,
feta cheese, smelts, girl scout cookies. At the Rendezvous
Room in Honolulu the Kid bolted 12,000 macadamia nuts and
67 bananas in less than an hour. During a Cubs-Phillies game
at Wrigley field he put away 43 hot dogs—with buns—and
112 Cokes. In Orkney it was legs of lamb; in Frankfurt, Em-
mentaler and schnitzel; in Kiev, pirogen. He was irrepress-
ible. In Stelton, New Jersey, he finished off 6 gallons of
borscht and 93 four-ounce jars of gefilte fish while sitting atop
a flagpole. The press ate it up.
Toward the end of the New Jersey session a reporter from
ABC Sports swung a boom mike up to where the Kid sat on
his eminence, chewing the last of the gefilte fish. "What are
your plans for the future, Kid?" shouted the newsman.
"I'm after the Big One," the Kid replied.
"Angelo D.?"
The camera zoomed in, the Kid grinned.

"Capocollo, chili and curry,
Big Man, you better start to worry."

Angelo was rattled. He gave up the morning paper and
banned the use of the Kid's name around the Training Table.

Kid Gullet: every time he heard those three syllables his stomach clenched. Now he lay on the bed, the powerful digestive machinery tearing away at breakfast, a bag of peanuts in his hand, his mind sifting through the tough bouts and spectacular triumphs of the past. There was Beau Riviere from Baton Rouge, who nearly choked him on deep-fried mud puppies, and Pinky Luzinski from Pittsburgh, who could gulp down 300 raw eggs and then crunch up the shells as if they were potato chips. Or the Japanese sumo wrestler who swallowed marbles by the fistful and throve on sashimi in a fiery mustard sauce. He'd beaten them all, because he had grit and determination and talent—and he would beat this kid too. Angelo sat up and roared: "I'm still the champ!"

The door cracked open. It was Decoud. "That's the spirit, Killer. Remember D. D. Peloris, Max Manger, Bozo Miller, Spoonbill Rizzo? Bums. All of them. You beat 'em, Champ."

"Yeah!" Angelo bellowed. "And I'm going to flatten this Gullet too."

"That's the ticket: leave him gasping for Bromo."

"They'll be pumping his stomach when I'm through with him."

Out in L.A. the Kid was taking on Turk Harris, number one contender for the heavyweight crown. The Kid's style was Tabasco and Worcestershire; Harris was a mashed-potato and creamed-corn man—a trencherman of the old school. Like Angelo D.

Harris opened with a one-two combination of rice and kidney beans; the Kid countered with cocktail onions and capers. Then Harris hit him with baklava—400 two-inch squares of it. The Kid gobbled them like hors d'oeuvres, came back with chili rellenos and asparagus vinaigrette. He KO'd Harris in the middle of the fourth round. After the bout he stood in a circle of jabbing microphones, flashing lights. "I got one thing

to say," he shouted. "And if you're out there, Big Man, you
better take heed:

> I'm going to float like a parfait,
> Sting like a tamale.
> Big Man, you'll hit the floor,
> In four."

At the preliminary weigh-in for the title bout the Kid
showed up on roller skates in a silver lamé jumpsuit. He
looked like something off the launching pad at Cape Canav-
eral. Angelo, in his coal-bucket trousers and suspenders,
could have been mistaken for an aging barber or a boccie
player strayed in from the park.

The Kid had a gallon jar of hot cherry peppers under his
arm. He wheeled up to the Champ, bolted six or seven in
quick succession, and then held one out to him by the stem.
"Care for an appetizer, Pops?" Angelo declined, his face dour
and white, the big fleshy nostrils heaving like a stallion's.
Then the photographers posed the two, belly to belly. In the
photograph, which appeared on the front page of the paper
the following morning, Angelo D. looked like an advertisement for heartburn.

There was an SRO crowd at the Garden for the title bout.
Scalpers were getting two hundred and up for tickets. ABC
Sports was there, Colonel Sanders was there, Arthur
Treacher, Julia Child, James Beard, Ronald McDonald,
Mamma Leone. It was the Trenching Event of the Century.

Spider Decoud and the Kid's manager had inspected the
ring and found the arrangements to their satisfaction—each
man had a table, stool, stack of plates and cutlery. Linen
napkins, a pitcher of water. It would be a fourteen-round
affair, each round going ten minutes with a sixty-second bell

break. The contestants would name their dishes for alternate rounds, the Kid, as challenger, leading off.

A hush fell over the crowd. And then the chant, rolling from back to front like breakers washing the beach: GULLET, GULLET, GULLET! There he was, the Kid, sweeping down the aisle like a born champion in his cinnamon-red robe with the silver letters across the abdomen. He stepped into the ring, clasped his hands, and shook them over his head. The crowd roared like rock faces slipping deep beneath the earth. Then he did a couple of deep knee bends and sat down on his stool. At that moment Angelo shuffled out from the opposite end of the arena, stern, grim, raging, the tight curls at the back of his neck standing out like the tail feathers of an albatross, his barren dome ghostly under the klieg lights, the celebrated paunch swelling beneath his opalescent robe like a fat wad of butterball turkeys. The crowd went mad. They shrieked, hooted and whistled, women kissed the hem of his gown, men reached out to pat his bulge. ANGELO! He stepped into the ring and took his seat as the big black mike descended from the ceiling.

The announcer, in double lapels and bow tie, shouted over the roar, "Ladies and Gentlemen—", while Angelo glared at the Kid, blood in his eye. He was choked with a primordial competitive fury, mad as a kamikaze, deranged with hunger. Two days earlier Decoud had lured him into a deserted meat locker and bolted the door—and then for the entire forty-eight hours had projected pornographic food films on the wall. Fleshy wet lips closing on éclairs, zoom shots of masticating teeth, gulping throats, probing tongues, children innocently sucking at Tootsie Roll pops—it was obscene, titillating, maddening. And through it all a panting soundtrack composed of grunts and sighs and the smack of lips. Angelo D. climbed into the ring a desperate man. But even money nonetheless. The Kid gloated in his corner.

"At this table, in the crimson trunks," bellowed the announcer, "standing six foot two inches tall and weighing in at
three hundred and seventy-seven pounds . . . is the challenger, Kid Gullet!" A cheer went up, deafening. The announcer pointed to Angelo. "And at this table, in the pearly
trunks and standing five foot seven and a half inches tall and
weighing in at three hundred and twenty-three pounds," he
bawled, his voice rumbling like a cordon of cement trucks, "is
the Heavyweight Champion of the World . . . Angelo D.!"
Another cheer, perhaps even louder. Then the referee took
over. He had the contestants step to the center of the ring,
the exposed flesh of their chests and bellies like a pair of
avalanches, while he asked if each was acquainted with the
rules. The Kid grinned like a shark. "All right then," the ref
said, "touch midriffs and come out eating."

The bell rang for Round One. The Kid opened with
Szechwan hot and sour soup, three gallons. He lifted the
tureen to his lips and slapped it down empty. The Champ
followed suit, his face aflame, sweat breaking out on his
forehead. He paused three times, and when finally he set the
tureen down he snatched up the water pitcher and drained it
at a gulp while the crowd booed and Decoud yelled from the
corner: "Lay off the water or you'll bloat up like a blowfish!"
Angelo retaliated with clams on the half shell in Round
Two: 512 in ten minutes. But the Kid kept pace with him—
and as if that weren't enough, he sprinkled his own portion
with cayenne pepper and Tabasco. The crowd loved it. They
gagged on their hot dogs, pelted the contestants with plastic
cups and peanut shells, gnawed at the backs of their seats.
Angelo looked up at the Kid's powerful jaws, the lips stained
with Tabasco, and began to feel queasy.
The Kid staggered him with lamb curry in the next round.
The crowd was on its feet, the Champ's face was green, the

fork motionless in his hand, the ref counting down, Decoud twisting the towel in his fists—when suddenly the bell sounded and the Champ collapsed on the table. Decoud leaped into the ring, chafed Angelo's abdomen, sponged his face. "Hang in there, Champ," he said, "and come back hard with the carbohydrates."

Angelo struck back with potato gnocchi in Round Four; the Kid countered with Kentucky burgoo. They traded blows through the next several rounds, the Champ scoring with Nesselrode pie, fettucine Alfredo and poi, the Kid lashing back with jambalaya, shrimp creole and herring in horse-radish sauce.

After the bell ending Round Eleven, the bout had to be held up momentarily because of a disturbance in the audi-ence. Two men, thin as tapers and with beards like Spanish moss, had leaped into the ring waving posters that read RE-MEMBER BIAFRA. The Kid started up from his table and pinned one of them to the mat, while security guards nabbed the other. The Champ sat immobile on his stool, eyes tearing from the horseradish sauce, his fist clenched round the handle of the water pitcher. When the ring was cleared the bell rang for Round Twelve.

It was the Champ's round all the way: sweet potato pie with butterscotch syrup and pralines. For the first time the Kid let up—toward the end of the round he dropped his fork and took a mandatory eight count. But he came back strong in the thirteenth with a savage combination of Texas wieners and sauce diable. The Champ staggered, went down once, twice, flung himself at the water pitcher while the Kid gorged like a machine, wiener after wiener, blithely lapping the hot sauce from his fingers and knuckles with an epicurean relish. Then Angelo's head fell to the table, his huge whiskered jowl mired in a pool of béchamel and butter. The fans sprang to their feet, feinting left and right, snapping their jaws and yabbering for the kill. The Champ's eyes fluttered open, the ref counted over him.

It was then that it happened. His vision blurring, Angelo gazed out into the crowd and focused suddenly on the stooped and wizened figure of an old woman in a black bonnet. Decoud stood at her elbow. Angelo lifted his head. "Ma?" he said. "Eat, Angelo, eat!" she called, her voice a whisper in the apocalyptic thunder of the crowd. "Clean your plate!"

"Nine!" howled the referee, and suddenly the Champ came to life, lashing into the sauce diable like a crocodile. He bolted wieners, sucked at his fingers, licked the plate. Some say his hands moved so fast that they defied the eye, a mere blur, slapstick in double time. Then the bell rang for the final round and Angelo announced his dish: "Gruel!" he roared. The Kid protested. "What kind of dish is that?" he whined. "Gruel? Who ever heard of gruel in a championship bout?" But gruel it was. The Champ lifted the bowl to his lips, pasty ropes of congealed porridge trailing down his chest; the crowd cheered, the Kid toyed with his spoon—and then it was over.

The referee stepped in, helped Angelo from the stool and held his flaccid arm aloft. Angelo was plate-drunk, reeling. He looked out over the cheering mob, a welter of button heads like B in B mushrooms—or Swedish meatballs in a rich golden sauce. Then he gagged. "The winner," the ref was shouting, "and still champion, Angelo D.!"

We Are Norsemen

W E ARE NORSEMEN, hardy and bold. We mount the black waves in our doughty sleek ships and go a-raiding. We are Norsemen, tough as stone. At least some of us are. Myself, I'm a skald—a poet, that is. I go along with Thorkell Son of Thorkell the Misaligned and Kolbein Snub when they sack the Irish coast and violate the Irish children, women, dogs and cattle and burn the Irish houses and pitch the ancient priceless Irish manuscripts into the sea. Then I sing about it. Doggerel like this:

> Fell I not nor failed at
> Fierce words, but my piercing
> Blade mouth gave forth bloody
> Bane speech, its harsh teaching.

Catch the kennings? That's the secret of this skaldic verse—make it esoteric and shoot it full of kennings. Anyway, it's a living.

But I'm not here to carp about a skald's life, I'm here to
make art. Spin a tale for posterity. Weave a web of mystery.

That year the winter ran at us like a sword, October to May.
You know the sort of thing: permafrosting winds, record cold.
The hot springs crusted over, birds stiffened on the wing and
dropped to the earth like stones, Thorkell the Old froze to the
crossbar in the privy. Even worse: thin-ribbed wolves yab-
bered on our doorstep, chewed up our coats and boots, and
then—one snowy night—made off with Thorkell the Young. It
was impossible. We crouched round the fire, thatch leaking,
and froze our norns off. The days were short, the mead barrel
deep. We drank, shivered, roasted a joint, told tales. The fire
played off our faces, red-gold and amber, and we fastened on
the narrator's voice like a log on a dark sea, entranced, falling
in on ourselves, the soft cadences pulling us through the
waves, illuminating shorelines, battlefields, mountains of
plunder. Unfortunately, the voice was most often mine. Believe me, a winter like that a skald really earns his keep—six
months, seven days a week, and an audience of hard-bitten
critics with frost in their beards. The nights dragged on.

One bleak morning we saw that yellow shoots had begun to
stab through the cattle droppings in the yard—we stretched,
yawned, and began to fill our boats with harrying matériel.
We took our battle axes, our throwing axes, our hewing axes,
our massive stroke-dealing swords, our disemboweling
spears, a couple of strips of jerky and a jug of water. As I said,
we were tough. Some of us wore our twin-horned battle helmets, the sight of which interrupts the vital functions of our
victims and enemies and inspires high-keyed vibrato. Others
of us, in view of fifteen-degree temperatures and a stiff breeze
whitening the peaks of the waves, felt that the virtue of

toughness had its limits. I decided on a lynx hat that gave elaborate consideration to the ears.

We fought over the gravel brake to launch our terrible swift ship. The wind shrieked of graves robbed, the sky was a hearth gone cold. An icy froth soaked us to the waist. Then we were off, manning the oars in smooth Nordic sync, the ship lurching through rocky breakers, heaving up, slapping down. The spray shot needles in our eyes, the oars lifted and dipped. An hour later the mainland winked into oblivion behind the dark lids of sea and sky.

There were thirteen of us: Thorkell Son of Thorkell the Misaligned, Thorkell the Short, Thorkell Thorkellsson, Thorkell Cat, Thorkell Flat-Nose, Thorkell-neb, Thorkell Ale-Lover, Thorkell the Old, Thorkell the Deep-minded, Ofeig, Skeggi, Grim and me. We were tough. We were hardy. We were bold.

Nonetheless the voyage was a disaster. A northeaster roared down on us like a herd of drunken whales and swept us far off course. We missed our landfall—Ireland—by at least two hundred miles and carried past into the open Atlantic. Eight weeks we sailed, looking for land. Thorkell the Old was bailing one gray afternoon and found three menhaden in his bucket. We ate them raw. I speared an albatross and hung it round my neck. It was no picnic.

Then one night we heard the cries of gulls like souls stricken in the dark. Thorkell Ale-Lover, keen of smell, snuffed the breeze. "Landfall near," he said. In the morning the sun threw our shadows on a new land—buff and green, slabs of gray, it swallowed the horizon.

"Balder be praised!" said Thorkell the Old.

"Thank Frigg," I said.

We skirted the coast, looking for habitations to sack. There were none. We'd discovered a wasteland. The Thorkells were for putting ashore to replenish our provisions and make sacrifice to the gods (in those days we hadn't yet learned to swallow unleavened bread and dab our foreheads with ashes. We were real primitives.) We ran our doughty sleek warship up a sandy spit and leaped ashore, fierce as flayed demons. It was an unnecessary show of force, as the countryside was desolate, but it did our hearts good.

The instant my feet touched earth the poetic fit came on me and I composed this verse:

> New land, new-found beyond
> The mickle waves by fell
> Men-fish, their stark battle
> Valor failèd them not.

No *Edda*, I grant you—but what can you expect after six weeks of bailing? I turned to Thorkell Son of Thorkell the Misaligned, my brain charged with creative fever. "Hey!" I shouted, "let's name this new-found land!" The others crowded round. Thorkell Son of Thorkell the Misaligned looked down at me (he was six four, his red beard hung to his waist). "We'll call it—Newfoundland!" I roared. There was silence. The twin horns of Thorkell's helmet pierced the sky, his eyes were like stones. "Thorkell-land," he said.

We voted. The Thorkells had it, 9 to 4.

For two and a half weeks we plumbed the coast, catching conies, shooting deer, pitching camp on islands or guarded promontories. I'd like to tell you it was glorious—golden sunsets, virgin forests, the thrill of discovery and all that—but when your business is sacking and looting, a virgin forest is the last thing you want to see. We grumbled bitterly. But

Thorkell Son of Thorkell the Misaligned was loath to admit that the land to which he'd given his name was uninhabited—and consequently of no use whatever. We forged on. Then one morning he called out from his place at the tiller: "Hah!" he said, and pointed toward a rocky abutment a hundred yards ahead. The mist lay on the water like flocks of sheep. I craned my neck, squinted, saw nothing. And then suddenly, like a revelation, I saw them: three tall posts set into the earth and carved with the figures of men and beasts. The sight brought water to my eyes and verse to my lips (but no sense in troubling you with any dilatory stanzas now—this is a climactic moment).

We landed. Crept up on the carvings, sly and wary, silent as stones. As it turned out, our caution was superfluous: the place was deserted. Besides the carvings (fanged monsters, stags, serpents, the grinning faces of a new race) there was no evidence of human presence whatever. Not even a footprint. We hung our heads: another bootyless day. Ofeig—the berserker—was seized with his berserker's rage and wound up hacking the three columns to splinters with his massive stroke-dealing sword.

The Thorkells were of the opinion that we should foray inland in search of a village to pillage. Who was I to argue? Inland we went, ever hardy and bold, up hill and down dale, through brakes and brambles and bogs and clouds of insects that rushed up our nostrils and down our throats. We found nothing. On the way back to the ship we were luckier. Thorkell-neb stumbled over a shadow in the path, and when the shadow leaped up and shot through the trees, we gave chase. After a good rib-heaving run we caught what proved to be a boy, eleven or twelve, his skin the color of copper, the feathers of birds in his hair. Like the Irish, he spoke gibberish.

Thorkell Son of Thorkell the Misaligned drew pictures in the sand and punched the boy in the chest until the boy

agreed to lead us to his people, the carvers of wood. We were
Norsemen, and we always got our way. All of us warmed to
the prospect of spoils, and off we went on another trek. We
brought along our short-swords and disemboweling
spears—just in case—though judging from the boy's condition
(he was bony and naked, his eyes deep and black as the spaces
between the stars) we had nothing to fear from his kindred.

We were right. After tramping through the under- and
overgrowth for half an hour we came to a village: smoking
cook pots, skinny dogs, short and ugly savages, their hair the
color of excrement. I counted six huts of branches and mud,
the sort of thing that might excite a beaver. When we stepped
into the clearing—tall, hardy and bold—the savages set up a
fiendish caterwauling and rushed for their weapons. But what
a joke their weapons were! Ofeig caught an arrow in the air,
looked at the head on it, and collapsed laughing: it was made
of flint. Flint. Can you believe it? Here we'd come Frigg
knows how many miles for plunder and the best we could do
was a bunch of Stone Age aborigines who thought that a
necklace of dogs' teeth was the height of fashion. Oh how we
longed for those clever Irish and their gold brooches and
silver-inlaid bowls. Anyway, we subdued these screechers as
we called them, sacrificed the whole lot of them to the gods
(the way I saw it we were doing them a favor), and headed
back to our terrible swift ship, heavy of heart. There was no
longer any room for debate: Ireland, look out!

As we pointed the prow east the westering sun threw the
shadow of the new land over us. Thorkell the Old looked back
over his shoulder and shook his head in disgust. "That
place'll never amount to a hill of beans," he said.

And then it was gone.

Days rose up out of the water and sank behind us. Intrepid
Norsemen, we rode the currents, the salt breeze tickling our

nostrils and bellying the sail. Thorkell Flat-Nose was our
navigator. He kept two ravens on a cord. After five and a half
weeks at sea he released one of them and it shot off into the
sky and vanished—but in less than an hour the bird was spotted off starboard, winging toward us, growing larger by turns
until finally it flapped down on the prow and allowed its leg to
be looped to the cord. Three days later Flat-Nose released the
second raven. The bird mounted high, winging to the south-
east until it became a black rune carved into the horizon. We
followed it into a night of full moon, the stars like milk splat-
tered in the cauldron of the sky. The sea whispered at the
prow, the tiller hissed behind us. Suddenly Thorkell Ale-
Lover cried, "Land-ho!" We were fell and grim and ravenous.
We looked up at the black ribbon of the Irish coast and
grinned like wolves. Our shoulders dug at the oars, the sea
sliced by. An hour later we landed.

Ofeig was for sniffing out habitations, free-booting and laying waste. But dawn crept on apace, and Thorkell Son of
Thorkell the Misaligned reminded him that we Norsemen
attack only under cover of darkness, swift and silent as a
nightmare. Ofeig did not take it well: the berserker's rage
came on him and he began to froth and chew at his tongue and
howl like a skinned beast. It was a tense moment. We backed
off as he grabbed for his battle-ax and whirred it about his
head. Fortunately he stumbled over a root and began to attack
the earth, gibbering and slavering, sparks slashing out from
buried stones as if the ground had suddenly caught fire. (Ad-
mittedly, berserkers can be tough to live with—but you can't
beat them when it comes to seizing hearts with terror or
battling trolls, demons or demiurges.)

Our reaction to all this was swift and uncomplicated: we
moved up the beach about two hundred yards and settled
down to get some rest. I stretched out in a patch of wildflowers and watched the sky, Ofeig's howls riding the breeze like a

celestial aria, waves washing the shore. The Thorkells slept on
their feet. It was nearly light when we finally dozed off, vi-
sions of plunder dancing in our heads.

I woke to the sound of whetstone on ax: we were polishing
the blade edges of our fearsome battle weapons. It was late
afternoon. We hadn't eaten in days. Thorkell-neb and Skeggi
stood naked on the beach, basting one another with black
mud scooped from a nearby marsh. I joined them. We darkened our flaxen hair, drew grim black lines under our eyes,
chanted fight songs. The sun hit the water like a halved fruit,
then vanished. A horned owl shot out across the dunes.
Crickets kreeked in the bushes. The time had come. We
drummed one another about the neck and shoulders for a
while ("Yeah!" we yelled, "yeah!"), fastened our helmets, and
then raced our serpent-headed ship into the waves.

A few miles up the coast we came on a light flickering out
over the dark corrugations of the sea. As we drew closer it
became apparent that the source of light was detached from
the coast itself—could it be an island? Our blood quickened,
our lips drew back in anticipation. Ravin and rapine at last!
And an island no less—what could be more ideal? There
would be no escape from our pure silent fury, no chance of
secreting treasures, no hope of reinforcements hastily roused
from bumpkin beds in the surrounding countryside. Ha!

An island it was—a tiny point of land, slick with ghostly
cliffs and crowned with the walls of a monastery. We circled
it, shadows on the dark swell. The light seemed to emanate
from a stone structure atop the highest crag—some bookish
monk with his nose to the paper no doubt, copying by the last
of the firelight. He was in for a surprise. We rode the bosom
of the sea and waited for the light to fail. Suddenly Thorkell
the Old began to cackle. "That'll be Inishmurray," he
wheezed. "Fattest monastery on the west coast." Our eyes

glowed. He spat into the spume."Thought it looked familiar,"
he said. "I helped Thorir Paunch sack it back in '75." Then the
light died and the world became night.

We watched the bookish monk in our minds' eyes: kissing
the text and laying it on a shelf, scattering the fire, plodding
wearily to his cell and the cold gray pallet. I recited an incen-
diary verse while we waited for the old ecclesiast to tumble
into sleep:

> Eye-bleed monk,
> Night his bane.
> Darkness masks
> The sea-wound,
> Mickle fell,
> Mickle stark.

I finished the recitation with a flourish, rolling the mickles
like thunder. Then we struck.

It was child's play. The slick ghostly cliffs were like rolling
meadows, the outer wall a branch in our path. There was no
sentry, no watchdog, no alarm. We dropped down into the
courtyard, naked, our bodies basted black, our doughty
death-dealing weapons in hand. We were shadows, fears,
fragments of a bad dream.

Thorkell Son of Thorkell the Misaligned stole into one of the
little stone churches and emerged with a glowing brand. Then
he set fire to two or three of the wickerwork cells and a pile of
driftwood. From that point on it was pandemonium—Ofeig
tumbling stone crosses, the Thorkells murdering monks in
their beds, Skeggi and Thorkell the Old chasing women,
Thorkell Ale-Lover waving joints of mutton and horns of beer.
The Irish defended themselves as best they could, two or
three monks coming at us with barbed spears and pilgrim's

staffs, but we made short work of them. We were Norsemen, after all.

For my own part, I darted here and there through the smoke and rubble, seized with a destructive frenzy, frightening women and sheep with my hideous blackened features, cursing like a jay. I even cut down a doddering crone for the sake of a gold brooch, my sweetheart Thorkella in mind. Still, despite the lust and chaos and the sweet smell of anarchy, I kept my head and my poet's eye. I observed each of the principal Thorkells with a reporter's acuity, noting each valorous swipe and thrust, the hot skaldic verses already forming on my lips. But then suddenly I was distracted: the light had reappeared in the little chapel atop the crag. I counted Thorkells (no mean feat when you consider the congeries of legs and arms, sounds and odors, the panicked flocks of sheep, pigs and chickens, the jagged flames, the furious womanizing, gormandizing and sodomizing of the crew). As I say, I counted Thorkells. We were all in sight. Up above, the light grew in intensity, flaming like a planet against the night sky. I thought of the bookish monk and started up the hill.

The night susurrated around me: crickets, katydids, cicadas, and far below the rush of waves on the rocks. The glare from the fires behind me gave way to blackness, rich and star-filled. I hurried up to the chapel, lashed by malice aforethought and evil intent—bookish monk, bookish monk—and burst through the door. I was black and terrible, right down to the tip of my foreskin. "Arrrrr!" I growled. The monk sat at a table, his hands clenched, head bent over a massive tome. He was just as I'd pictured him: pale as milk, a fringe of dark pubic hair around his tonsure, puny and frail. He did not look up. I growled again, and when I got no response I began to slash at candles and pitchers and icons and all the other superstitious trappings of the place. Pottery splashed to the floor, shelves tumbled. Still he bent over the book.

The book. What in Frigg's name was a book anyway? Scratchings on a sheet of cowhide. Could you fasten a cloak with it, carry mead in it, impress women with it, wear it in your hair? There was gold and silver scattered round the room, and yet he sat over the book as if it could glow or talk or something. The idiot. The pale, puny, unhardy, unbold idiot. A rage came over me at the thought of it—I shoved him aside and snatched up the book, thick pages, dark characters, the mystery and magic. Snatched it up, me, a poet, a Norseman, an annihilator, an illiterate. Snatched it up and watched the old monk's suffering features as I fed it, page by filthy page, into the fire. Ha!

We are Norsemen, hardy and bold. We mount the black waves in our doughty sleek ships and we go a-raiding. We are Norsemen, tough as stone. We are Norsemen.

Heart of a Champion

W E SCAN THE CORNFIELDS and the wheatfields winking gold and goldbrown and yellowbrown in the midday sun, on up the grassy slope to the barn redder than red against the sky bluer than blue, across the smooth stretch of the barnyard with its pecking chickens, and then right on up to the screen door at the back of the house. The door swings open, a black hole in the sun, and Timmy emerges with his corn-silk hair, corn-fed face. He is dressed in crisp overalls, striped T-shirt, stubby blue Keds. There'd have to be a breeze—and we're not disappointed—his clean fine cup-cut hair waves and settles as he scuffs across the barnyard and out to the edge of the field. The boy stops there to gaze out over the nodding wheat, eyes unsquinted despite the sun, and blue as tinted lenses. Then he brings three fingers to his lips in a neat triangle and whistles long and low, sloping up sharp to cut off at the peak. A moment passes: he whistles

again. And then we see it—way out there at the far corner of
the field—the ripple, the dashing furrow, the blur of the
streaking dog, white chest, flashing feet.

They're in the woods now. The boy whistling, hands in
pockets, kicking along with his short baby-fat strides; the dog
beside him wagging the white tip of her tail like an all-clear
flag. They pass beneath an arching old black-barked oak. It
creaks. And suddenly begins to fling itself down on them:
immense, brutal: a panzer strike. The boy's eyes startle and
then there's a blur, a smart snout clutching his pantleg, the
thunderblast of the trunk, the dust and spinning leaves.
"Golly, Lassie . . . I didn't even see it," says the boy sitting
safe in a mound of moss. The collie looks up at him (the svelte
snout, the deep gold logician's eyes), and laps at his face.

And now they're down by the river. The water is brown
with angry suppurations, spiked with branches, fence posts,
tires and logs. It rushes like the sides of boxcars—and chews
deep and insidious at the bank under Timmy's feet. The roar
is like a jetport: little wonder he can't hear the dog's warning
bark. We watch the crack appear, widen to a ditch; then the
halves separating (snatch of red earth, writhe of worm), the
poise and pitch, and Timmy crushing down with it. Just a
flash—but already he's way downstream, his head like a plastic jug, dashed and bobbed, spinning toward the nasty mouth
of the falls. But there's the dog—fast as a struck match—
bursting along the bank all white and gold melded in motion,
hair sleeked with the wind of it, legs beating time to the
panting score. . . . Yet what can she hope to do?—the current surges on, lengths ahead, sure bet to win the race to the
falls. Timmy sweeps closer, sweeps closer, the falls loud now
as a hundred tympani, the war drums of the Sioux, Africa
gone bloodlust mad! The dog strains, lashing over the wet

earth like a whipcrack; strains every last ganglion and dendrite until finally she draws abreast of him. Then she's in the air, the foaming yellow water. Her paws churning like pistons, whiskers chuffing with the exertion—oh the roar!—and there, she's got him, her sure jaws clamping down on the shirt collar, her eyes fixed on the slip of rock at the falls' edge. Our blood races, organs palpitate. The black brink of the falls, the white paws digging at the rock—and then they're safe. The collie sniffs at Timmy's inert little form, nudges his side until she manages to roll him over. Then clears his tongue and begins mouth-to-mouth.

Night: the barnyard still, a bulb burning over the screen door. Inside, the family sit at dinner, the table heaped with pork chops, mashed potatoes, applesauce and peas, a pitcher of clean white milk. Home-baked bread. Mom and Dad, their faces sexless, bland, perpetually good-humored and sympathetic, poise stiff-backed, forks in midswoop, while Timmy tells his story: "So then Lassie grabbed me by the collar and golly I musta blanked out cause I don't remember anything more till I woke up on the rock—"

"Well I'll be," says Mom.

"You're lucky you've got such a good dog, son," says Dad, gazing down at the collie where she lies patiently, snout over paw, tail wapping the floor. She is combed and washed and fluffed, her lashes mascaraed and curled, her chest and paws white as dishsoap. She looks up humbly. But then her ears leap, her neck jerks round—and she's up at the door, head cocked, alert. A high yipping yowl like a stuttering fire whistle shudders through the room. And then another. The dog whines.

"Darn," says Dad. "I thought we were rid of those coyotes—next thing they'll be after the chickens again."

The moon blanches the yard, leans black shadows on the trees, the barn. Upstairs in the house, Timmy lies sleeping in the pale light, his hair fastidiously mussed, his breathing gentle. The collie lies on the throw rug beside the bed. We see that her eyes are open. Suddenly she rises and slips to the window, silent as a shadow. And looks down the long elegant snout to the barnyard below, where the coyote slinks from shade to shade, a limp pullet dangling from his jaws. He is stunted, scabious, syphilitic, his forepaw trap-twisted, his eyes running. The collie whimpers softly from behind the window. And the coyote stops in mid-trot, frozen in a cold shard of light, ears high on his head. Then drops the chicken at his feet, leers up at the window and begins a soft, crooning, sad-faced song.

The screen door slaps behind Timmy as he bolts from the house, Lassie at his heels. Mom's head emerges on the rebound. "Timmy!" (He stops as if jerked by a rope, turns to face her.) "You be home before lunch, hear?"

"Sure, Mom," he says, already spinning off, the dog by his side. We get a close-up of Mom's face: she is smiling a benevolent boys-will-be-boys smile. Her teeth are perfect.

In the woods Timmy steps on a rattler and the dog bites its head off. "Gosh," he says. "Good girl, Lassie." Then he stumbles and slips over an embankment, rolls down the brushy incline and over a sudden precipice, whirling out into the breathtaking blue space like a sky diver. He thumps down on a narrow ledge twenty feet below. And immediately scrambles to his feet, peering timorously down the sheer wall to the heap of bleached bone at its base. Small stones break loose, shoot out like asteroids. Dirt-slides begin. But Lassie yarps reassuringly from above, sprints back to the barn for a winch and cable, hoists the boy to safety.

On their way back for lunch Timmy leads them through a

still and leaf-darkened copse. We remark how odd it is that the birds and crickets have left off their cheeping, how puzzling that the background music has begun to rumble so. Suddenly, round a bend in the path before them, the coyote appears. Nose to the ground, intent, unaware of them. But all at once he jerks to a halt, shudders like an epileptic, the hackles rising, tail dipping between his legs. The collie too stops short, just yards away, her chest proud and shaggy and white. The coyote cowers, bunches like a cat, glares at them. Timmy's face sags with alarm. The coyote lifts his lip. But then, instead of leaping at her adversary's throat, the collie prances up and stretches her nose out to him, her eyes soft as a leading lady's, round as a doe's. She's balsamed and perfumed; her full chest tapers a lovely S to her sleek haunches and sculpted legs. He is puny, runted, half her size, his coat like a discarded doormat. She circles him now, sniffing. She whimpers, he growls: throaty and tough, the bad guy. And stands stiff while she licks at his whiskers, noses at his rear, the bald black scrotum. Timmy is horror-struck. Then, the music sweeping off in birdtrills of flute and harpstring, the coyote slips round behind, throat thrown back, black lips tight with anticipation.

"What was she doing, Dad?" Timmy asks over his milk and sandwich.

"The sky was blue today, son," he says.

"But she had him trapped, Dad—they were stuck together end to end and I thought we had that wicked old coyote but then she went and let him go—what's got into her, Dad?"

"The barn was red today, son," he says.

Late afternoon: the sun mellow, more orange than white. Purpling clots of shadow hang from the branches, ravel out from the tree trunks. Bees and wasps and flies saw away at the wet full-bellied air. Timmy and the dog are far out beyond the north pasture, out by the old Indian burial mound, where the boy stoops now to search for arrowheads. Oddly, the collie is not watching him: instead she's pacing the crest above, whimpering softly, pausing from time to time to stare out across the forest, her eyes distant and moonstruck. Behind her, storm clouds squat on the horizon like dark kidneys or brains.

We observe the wind kicking up: leaves flapping like wash, saplings quivering, weeds whipping. It darkens quickly now, the clouds scudding low and smoky over the treetops, blotting the sun from view. Lassie's white is whiter than ever, highlighted against the dark horizon, the wind-whipped hair foaming around her. Still she doesn't look down at the boy: he digs, dirty-kneed, stoop-backed, oblivious. Then the first fat random drops, a flash, the volcanic blast of thunder. Timmy glances over his shoulder at the noise: he's just in time to watch the scorched pine plummeting toward the constellated freckles in the center of his forehead. Now the collie turns—too late!—the *swoosh-whack!* of the tree, the trembling needles. She's there in an instant, tearing at the green welter, struggling through to his side. He lies unconscious in the muddying earth, hair artistically arranged, a thin scratch painted on his cheek. The trunk lies across the small of his back like the tail of a brontosaurus. The rain falls.

Lassie tugs doggedly at a knob in the trunk, her pretty paws slipping in the wet—but it's no use—it would take a block and tackle, a crane, an army of Bunyans to shift that stubborn bulk. She falters, licks at his ear, whimpers. We observe the troubled look in her eye as she hesitates, uncertain, priorities warring: should she stand guard, or dash for help? The decision is sure and swift—her eyes firm with purpose and she's off like a shard of shrapnel, already up the hill, shooting past the dripping trees, over the river, already cleaving through the high wet banks of wheat.

A moment later she's dashing through the puddled and rain-screened barnyard, barking right on up to the back door, where she pauses to scratch daintily, her voice high-pitched and insistent. Mom swings open the door and the collie pads in, claws clacking on the shiny linoleum. "What is it girl? What's the matter? Where's Timmy?"

"Yarf! Yarfata-yarf-yarf!"

"Oh my! Dad! Dad, come quickly!"

Dad rushes in, his face stolid and reassuring as the Lincoln Memorial. "What is it, dear? . . . Why, Lassie?"

"Oh Dad, Timmy's trapped under a pine tree out by the old Indian burial ground—"

"Arpit-arp."

"—a mile and a half past the north pasture."

Dad is quick, firm, decisive. "Lassie—you get back up there and stand watch over Timmy . . . Mom and I'll go for Doc Walker. Hurry now!"

The collie hesitates at the door: "Rarf-arrar-ra!"

"Right," says Dad. "Mom, fetch the chain saw."

We're back in the woods now. A shot of the mud-running burial mound locates us—yes, there's the fallen pine, and there: Timmy. He lies in a puddle, eyes closed, breathing slow. The hiss of the rain is loud as static. We see it at work: scattering leaves, digging trenches, inciting streams to swallow their banks. It lies deep now in the low areas, and in the mid areas, and in the high areas. Then a shot of the dam, some indeterminate (but short we presume) distance off, the yellow water churning over its lip like urine, the ugly earthen belly distended, blistered with the pressure. Raindrops pock the surface like a plague.

Suddenly the music plunges to those thunderous crouching chords—we're back at the pine now—what is it? There: the coyote. Sniffing, furtive, the malicious eyes, the crouch and slink. He stiffens when he spots the boy—but then slouches closer, a rubbery dangle drooling from between his mis-meshed teeth. Closer. Right over the prone figure now, those ominous chords setting up ominous vibrations in our bowels. He stoops, head dipping between his shoulders, irises caught in the corners of his eyes: wary, sly, predatory: the vulture slavering over the fallen fawn.

But wait!—here comes the collie, sprinting out of the wheatfield, bounding rock to rock across the crazed river, her limbs contourless with sheer speed and purpose, the music racing in a mad heroic prestissimo!

The jolting front seat of a Ford. Dad, Mom and the Doctor, all dressed in rain slickers and flap-brimmed rain hats, sitting shoulder to shoulder behind the clapping wipers. Their jaws set with determination, eyes aflicker with pioneer gumption.

The coyote's jaws, serrated grinders, work at the tough bone and cartilage of Timmy's left hand. The boy's eyelids flutter with the pain, and he lifts his head feebly—but almost immediately it slaps down again, flat and volitionless, in the mud. At that instant Lassie blazes over the hill like a cavalry charge, show-dog indignation aflame in her eyes. The scrag of a coyote looks up at her, drooling blood, choking down frantic bits of flesh. Looks up at her from eyes that go back thirty million years, savage and bloodlustful and free. Looks up un-moved, uncringing, the bloody snout and steady yellow eyes less a physical challenge than philosophical. We watch the collie's expression alter in midbound—the look of offended AKC morality giving way, dissolving. She skids to a halt,

drops her tail and approaches him, a buttery gaze in her
golden eyes. She licks the blood from his lips.

The dam. Impossibly swollen, rain festering the yellow
surface, a hundred new streams a minute rampaging in, the
pressure of those millions of gallons hard-punching those
millions more. There! the first gap, the water spewing out, a
burst bubo. And now the dam shudders, splinters, falls to
pieces like so much cheap pottery. The roar is devastating.

The two animals start at that terrible rumbling, and still
working their gummy jaws, they dash up the far side of the
hill. We watch the white-tipped tail retreating side by side
with the hacked and tick-blistered gray one—wagging like
raggled banners as they disappear into the trees at the top of
the rise. We're left with a tableau: the rain, the fallen pine in
the crotch of the valley's V, the spot of the boy's head. And
that chilling roar in our ears. Suddenly the wall of water appears at the far end of the V, smashing through the little
declivity like a god-sized fist, prickling with shattered trunks
and boulders, grinding along like a quick-melted glacier, like
planets in collision. We cut to Timmy: eyes closed, hair plas-
tered, his left arm looking as though it should be wrapped in
butcher's paper. How? we wonder. How will they ever get
him out of this? But then we see them—Mom, Dad and the
Doctor—struggling up that same rise, rushing with the fre-
netic music now, the torrent seething closer, booming and
howling. Dad launches himself in full charge down the hill-
side—but the water is already sweeping over the fallen pine,
lifting it like paper—there's a blur, a quick clip of a typhoon at
sea (is that a flash of blond hair?), and it's over. The valley is
filled to the top of the rise, the water ribbed and rushing like

the Colorado in adolescence. Dad's pants are wet to the crotch.

Mom's face, the Doctor's. Rain. And then the opening strains of the theme song, one violin at first, swelling in mournful mid-American triumph as the full orchestra comes in, tearful, beautiful, heroic, sweeping us up and out of the dismal rain, back to the golden wheatfields in the midday sun. The boy cups his hands to his mouth and pipes: "Laahh-sie! Laahh-sie!" And then we see it—way out there at the end of the field—the ripple, the dashing furrow, the blur of the streaking dog, white chest, flashing feet.

Bloodfall

IT STARTED ABOUT three-thirty, a delicate tapping at the windows, the sound of rain. No one noticed: the stereo was turned up full and Walt was thumping his bass along with it, the TV was going, they were all stoned, passing wine and a glowing pipe, singing along with the records, playing Botticelli and Careers and Monopoly, crunching crackers. I noticed. In that brief scratching silence between songs, I heard it—looked up at the window and saw the first red droplets huddled there, more falling between them. Gesh and Scott and Isabelle were watching TV with the sound off, digging the music, lighting cigarettes, tapping fingers and feet, laughing. On the low table were cheese, oranges, wine, shiny paperbacks, a hash pipe. Incense smoked from a pendant urn. The three dogs sprawled on the carpet by the fireplace, Siamese cats curled on the mantel, the bench, the chair. The red droplets quivered, were struck by other, larger drops falling atop them, and began a meandering course down the windowpane. Alice laughed from the kitchen. She and Amy were peeling vegetables, baking pies, uncanning baby smoked oysters and sturgeon for hors d'oeuvres, sucking on olive pits. The windows were streaked with red. The music was too loud. No one noticed. It was another day.

When I opened the door to investigate, the three dogs sprang up and ran to me, tails awag; they stopped at the door, sniffing. It was hissing down now, a regular storm: it streamed red from the gutter over the door, splashing my pantleg. The front porch smelled like raw hamburger. My white pants were spotted with red. The dogs inched out now, stretching their necks: they lapped at the red puddle on the doorstep. Their heads and muzzles were soon slick with it. I slammed the door on them and walked back into the living room. Gesh and Scott were passing the pipe. On the TV screen were pictures of starving children: distended bellies, eyes as big as their bony heads, spiders' arms and spiders' legs: someone was laughing in the kitchen. "Hey!" I shouted. "Do you dig what's happening outside?" Nobody heard me. The windows were smeared with red: it fell harder. Gesh looked up to pass the pipe. "What happened to you?" he said. "Cut yourself?"

"No," I said. "It's raining blood."

Gesh was in the shower when the TV screen went blank. Earlier, when everybody had crowded around the open door, holding out their hands to it as it dripped down from the eaves, wowing and cursing and exclaiming, Gesh had pushed through and stepped out, down the stairs and out under the maple tree. His white pants, shirt and shoes turned pinkish, then a fresh wet red, the color of life. "It's fantastic out here!" he yelled. We held back. In a minute or two he came back up the steps, his face a mosaic mortared in blood, the clotted hair stuck to his forehead. He looked like the aftermath of an accident, or a casualty of war. "How do I look?" he said, licking the wet red from his lips. "Like the Masque of the Red Death or something? Huh?" Scott was taking pictures with his Nikkormat. The smell when Gesh stepped in reminded me of a trip I took with my mom and dad when I was in the third grade. An educational trip. Every weekend we took an educational trip. We went to the slaughterhouse. Gesh smelled like that when he came in. Amy made him take a shower with baby shampoo and peppermint soap. She laid out a fresh white shirt and pants for him, and his white slippers. Scott ran downstairs to the darkroom to develop his pictures. Basically he does black and whites of slum kids in rakish hats giving him the finger; old slum women, their fingers stewed to the bone; old slum men, fingering port pints in their pockets. These he enlarges and frames, and hangs about the house. One of them hangs in the corner over Alice's Reclino Love-Chair with the dyed rabbit-fur cover; another hangs in the dining room over my 125-gallon aquarium. The rabbit fur is dyed black.

Walt took a break for a minute to change records and adjust the treble on his amp. In the ringing silence that ensued, we realized that the TV was emitting a thin high-pitched whistle. There was no picture. "What the fuck?" said Isabelle. She jumped up, flipped through the channels. All gray, all emitting the same whistle. Isabelle's eyes were bleared. "Let's try the radio!" she said. It too: the same insidious whine. "The phone!" she shouted. The phone hummed softly in her ear, my ear, Walt's ear, Amy's ear. It was the same sort of hum you get from an empty conch shell. "It's dead," I said. We stood there mute, staring at the receiver suspended from its cord, clickless and ringless. We theorized:

Maybe it's a National Emergency—
Maybe it's D-day—
Maybe it's the Nuclear Holocaust—
Maybe it's Judgment Day—

Maybe it's the Rockets they're sending up—
But we all suspected the soundness of these extrapolations.
Probably it was just some new form of pollution, and a few
wires down in the storm. Gesh appeared in fresh white,
smelling like a candy cane. He walked deliberately to the
pipe, thumbed in a chunk of hash, and sucked the flame of a
match through it. Isabelle, quickly sedated, picked out a
couple of albums and Walt ducked under the embroidered
shoulder strap of his bass—the blast of music sealed the room,
stopped the ticking at the panes. Alice brought in the hors
d'oeuvres, and a comforting smell of exotic dishes abubble in
the kitchen. I sat, smoked, and ate.

In the morning I slipped early from the warmth of the nest
(Alice's tender buttock, Gesh's hairy satyr's foot framed there
beneath the sheets), wrapped my white robe over my white
pajamas, stepped into my fluffy white slippers, and went
downstairs, as I always do on Saturdays, to watch cartoons.
My mind was a tabula rasa, wire-brushed with intoxicants; my
dreams had been of cool colors, the green of the forest, the
cerulean of the summer sky. In the living room, a pinkish
light suffused the slats of the blinds. The window was like
stained glass. In the early morning quiet, the red splashes
drummed against it. I was stunned; and all alone there, at that
early hour, frightened. Then I heard the scratching at the
door: the dogs had been out all night. Without thinking, I
opened the door and they rushed in, great living lumps of raw
flesh, skinned carcasses come to life, slick with blood, their
bellies bloated with it. "No, no, get down!" But they were
already up on their hind legs, pawing affectionately at me,
their fetid breath in my face. Their teeth were stained red,
blood hung even in the sockets of their eyes. "Get down,
Goddammit!" My robe, my pajamas, my fluffy white slippers
were ruined: the blood crept through the white cotton like a

stain in water. I kicked out at the dogs. They backed off and
shook themselves—a fine bloodmist spotted the walls, the
white rugs of the hallway, the potted plants. The dogs
grunted, eased themselves down and licked their paws. Blood
seeped from beneath them. I felt sick from the stink of it, and
so upset with the mess that tears began to crowd my eyes—
exasperated, hopeless tears. The hallway looked like a sacrifi-
cial altar, my arms like the gory High Priest's. I would wash
and go back to bed, face life later.

In the bathroom I stepped carefully out of my clothes in an
effort to avoid staining the bathmat. It was no use. Blood
oozed from the fluffy red slippers. I wiped my hands and face
on the lining of the robe, bundled everything together and
stuffed it into the hamper. Seven electric toothbrushes, seven
cups, and seven hotcombs hung on the rack over the sink. We
kept the seven electric shavers, each in its own carrying case,
stacked neatly in the cabinet. I stepped into the shower, the
tap of blood against the bathroom window loud in my ears,
and turned on hot, full force. Eyes pressed tight, face in the
spray, I luxuriated in the warm pure rush of the water. I'd
always taken a great deal of pleasure in showering and bathing, in being clean—it reminded me of my mom and the baths
she used to give, sponging my crotch, kissing my wet little
feet . . . but there was something wrong—that odor—good
God, it was in the water supply! Horrified, I leaped from the
shower. In the steamed-over mirror I was newborn, coated in
blood and mucus, pulled hot from the womb. Diluted blood
streamed down my body, puddled at my feet. I lifted the
toilet seat and puked into the red bowl. Hung my head and
puked: puked and cried, until Amy came down and found me
there.

Gesh sat back in the stuffed chair. He wore his white robe
with the gold monogram, and his slippers. The bloodfall

hammered on. "We've got to look at the precedents," he said. There was a pie and a soufflé in the oven. We were in the living room, sipping apricot nectar, munching buns. Alice, in the entrance hall with detergent and scrub brush, was muttering like Lady Macbeth over the carpet stains. "What precedents?" I asked.

"Like all of that shit that went down in Egypt about thirty-five hundred years ago."

Walt was tuning his bass: dzhzhzhzhtt. dzhzhzhzhtt. He picked a rumbling note or two and looked up. "You're thinking of frogs, brother. Millions of frogs. Frogs under the bed, frogs in the flour, frogs in your shoes, clammy frogs' flippers slapping at your ass when you take a shit."

"No, no—there was something about blood too, wasn't there?"

"Yeah," said Walt. "Christ turned it into water. Or was it wine?"

"You know what happened in Egypt?! You want to know?" My voice cracked. I was getting hysterical. A cat jumped into my lap. I tossed it over my shoulder. Everything in the room had a red cast, like when you put on those red cellophane glasses as a kid, to read 3D comic books.

Gesh was staring at me: "So what happened?"

"Never mind," I said.

Amy howled from the basement. "Hey you guys, guess what? The stuff is ankle-deep down here and it's ruining everything. Our croquet set, our camping equipment, our dollhouse!" The announcement depressed us all, even Gesh. "Let's blow a bowl of hash and forget about it," he suggested.

"Anyhow," said Walt, "it'll be good for the trees." And he started a bass riff with a deep throbbing note—the hum of it hung in the air even after the lights went out and the rest of his run had attenuated to a thin metallic whisper. "Hey!" he said. From the kitchen: "Oh shit!" A moment later, Isabelle came in wringing her hands. "Well. The breakfast's ruined. We've got a half-baked pie and a flat soufflé sitting in the oven. And a raw-eggy blob purporting to be eggnog in the blender."

There was a strange cast to the room now. Not the gloom-gray of a drizzly day, but a deep burgundy, like a bottle of wine.

"Well? What am I going to do with it all—give it to the dogs?"

The dogs glanced up briefly. Their hair was matted and brown with dried blood. They were not hungry.

Scott whined: "I'm hungry."

I was scared. I'd been scared all along, scared from the moment I'd noticed the first drops on the window. I looked at Gesh, our leader: he was grinning in that lurid light, sucking reflectively on the pipe. "Don't hassle it, Iz," he said. "Mark and me'll pop down to the deli and get some sandwiches."

"I don't want to go out there—I'll lose my lunch."

"Come on, don't be such a candy ass. Besides, it'll give us a chance to talk to somebody, find out what's going on." He stood up. "Come on Mark, get your boots."

Outside was incredible. Red sky, red trees, red horizon: the whole world, from the fence to the field to the mountains across the river, looked like the inside of some colossal organ. I felt like an undigested lump of food—Jonah in the belly of the whale. There was the stench of rotting meat. The bloodfall streamed down hard as hail. Under the eaves, on the porch, we were fooling with our rain hats, trying to get up the nerve to run for the car. Gesh too, I could see, was upset. Yesterday it had been a freak, today a plague. "Well, what do you think, bro—make a run for it?" he said.

We ran—down the steps and into the mud. I slipped and fell, while Gesh hustled off through the blinding downpour. It

was deeper now, lying about the low spots in nasty red-black
puddles. I could feel it seeping in, trickling down my leg,
inside the boot: warm, sticky, almost hot. The smell of pu-
trefaction nauseated me. I choked back the apricot nectar and
biscuits, struggled up, and ran for the car. When I got there
Gesh was standing beside the door, blooddrops thrashing
about him. "What about the seats?" he said. "If we stain 'em
with this shit, it'll never come off."

"Fuck it. Let's just get out of this—"

"I mean I got a lot of scratch invested in this here BMW,
bro—"

The wind-whipped blood flailed our yellow slickers,
dripped from the flapping brims of our silly yellow rain hats.
We both climbed in. The engine started smooth, like a vacuum cleaner; the wipers clapped to and fro; the windshield
smeared. "Let's drive to the desert . . . the Arizona desert,
and get away from this . . . shit," I said. My voice was weak. I
felt ill. Automatically I reached for the window. "Hey—what
the fuck you doing?" Gesh said. It streamed down the inside
of the glass, bubbled over the upholstered door, puddled in
the ashtray on the armrest. I rolled the window up. "I feel
sick," I said. "Well for Christ's sake, puke outside." I didn't.
The thought of hanging my head out in that insane unnatural
downpour brought it up right there. In the sealed compartment the bouquet of the vomit and stink of the mud-blood on
our shoes was insupportable. I retched again: then dry-
retched. "Oh shit," said Gesh.

"I'm going back in," I said, the edge of a whimper in my
voice.

Five minutes later, Gesh returned, cursing. Scott was on
his way out the door, three cameras strung round his neck, to
get some color slides of the dripping trees. "What's the matter," he said. "You back already?"

"Couldn't see a fucking thing. I got down the end of the

drive and smacked into the stone wall. The wipers are totally useless—they just smear the crap all over the windshield. It's like looking through a finger painting."

"So what happened to the car?"

"It's not too bad—I was only going about two miles an hour."

Alice emerged from the kitchen, a pair of lighted candles in her hand, egg-walking to avoid spilling the hot wax. "Gesh! Take your slicker off—you're dripping that shit all over the floor . . . Couldn't make it, huh?"

"No."

"What are we going to do for food?" she asked.

"Scoop it up!" Walt shouted from the living room. "Scoop it up and pour it into balloons. Make blood pudding."

I was sitting in a chair, weak, stinking, blood crusting the lines of my hands. "I'm fed up with it," I said. "I'm going up to lie down."

"Good idea," said Gesh. "Think I'll join you."

"Me too," said Alice. "Can't do anything here—can't even read or listen to music."

"Yeah," said Walt. "Good idea. Save me a pillow."

"Me too," said Amy.

Scott stepped from beneath the cameras, strung them across the back of my chair. He yawned. Isabelle said it would be better if we all went to bed. She expressed a hope that after a long nap things would somehow come to their senses.

I woke from fevered dreams (a tropical forest: me in jodhpurs and pith helmet—queasy-faced—sharing a draught of warm cow's blood and milk with tree-tall Masai warriors) to a rubicund dimness, and the gentle breathing of the rest of the crew. They loomed, a humpbacked mound in the bed beside me. My ears were keen. Still it beat on the roof, sloshed in the gutters. Downstairs, somewhere, I heard the

sound of running water, the easy soughing gurgle of a mountain stream. I sat up. Were we leaking? I slipped into Amy's
slippers, lit a candle, crept apprehensively down the stairs. I
searched the hallway, living room, dining room, kitchen,
bathroom: nothing. A cat began wailing somewhere. The
basement! The cat bolted out when I opened the door, peered
down the dark shaft of the stairway. The flood was up nearly to
the fifth step, almost four feet deep, I guessed, and more
churning audibly in. The stench was stifling. I slammed the
door. For the first time I thought of the dike: why 'sblood! if
the dike went—it must be straining at its foundations this very
minute! I envisioned us out there, heroically stacking
sandbags, the wind in our faces, whipping our hair back, the
rising level of the flood registered in our stoic eyes—then I
thought of the tepid plasma seething in my nose, my mouth,
my eyes, and felt ill.

Gesh came down the stairs, scratching himself sleepily.
"How's it?" he said. I advised him to take a look at the cellar.
He did. "Holy shit! We've got to do something—start making
barricades, strapping floatables together, evacuating women
and children—and dogs!" He paused. "I'm starving," he said.
"Let's go see what we got left, bro." From the kitchen I could
hear him taking inventory: "Two six-packs of warm Coke; a jar
of Skippy peanut butter, crunchy—no bread; ten cans of
stewed tomatoes; half a box of granola; a quart of brown rice;
one tin of baby smoked oysters. Not a fuck of a lot. Hey Mark,
join me in a late afternoon snack?"

"No thanks. I'm not hungry."

We sat around the darkened living room that night, a single
candle guttering, the sound of bloodfall ticking at the windows, the hiss of rapids rushing against the stone walls of the
house, an insidious sloshing in the basement. Seepage had
begun at the front door, and Isabelle had dumped a fifty-

pound bag of kitty litter there in an attempt to absorb the moisture. Atop that was a restraining dike of other absorbent materials: boxes of cake mix, back issues of *Cosmopolitan*, electric blankets, Italian dictionaries, throw pillows, three dogs, a box of Tampax. A similar barricade protected the basement door. When Gesh had last opened the window to look, the red current eddying against the house had reached almost to the windowsill. We were deeply concerned, hungry, bored.

"I'm bored," said Amy.

"I'm hungry," whined Scott. "And I'm sick of Coke. I want a hot cup of Mu tea."

"It stinks in here," carped Isabelle. "Reminds me of when I was fifteen, working in the meat department at the A & P."

"My teeth are gritty," Alice said. "Wish the water and the damned toothbrushes would work."

Blood began to drip from the windowsill in the far corner of the room. It puddled atop the thirty-six-inch Fisher speaker in the corner. One of the cats began to lap at it.

Walt paced the room, a man dislocated. Deprived of his bass, he was empty, devoid of spirit, devoid of personality. He was incapable now of contributing to our meaningful dialogue on the situation. Gesh, however, tried to amuse us, take our minds off it. He said it was just a simple case of old mother earth menstruating, and that by tomorrow, the last day of the moon's cycle, it would no doubt stop. He passed around a fifth of châteauneuf and a thin joint. The pool beneath the door began to spread across the floor, creeping, growing, fanning out to where we sat in a small circle, the candlelight catching the blood in our flared nostrils. Shocked silent, we watched its inexorable approach as it glided out from the barricade in fingerlike projections, seeking the lowest point. The lowest point, it appeared, was directly beneath the Naugahyde pillow upon which my buttocks rested.

Slowly, methodically, the bulbous finger of blood stretched toward me, pointed at me. When it was about a foot away, I stood. "I'm going to bed," I said. "I'm taking two Tuinals. Try not to wake me."

It was morning when I woke. Gesh sat in a chair beside the bed, smoking a cigarette. The others slept. "It stopped," he said. He was right: the only sound was a sporadic drip-drip beyond the windows, a poststorm runoff. The celestial phlebotomy had ceased. "Good," was all I could manage. But I was elated, overjoyed, secure again! Life returned to normal!

"Hey—let's slip down to the deli and get some sandwiches and doughnuts and coffee and shit, sneak back, and surprise the rest of the crew," Gesh said.

Curiosity stirred me, and hunger too. But my stomach curdled at the thought of the gore and the stink, the yard like a deserted battlefield. I stared down at my pajama sleeve. Amy's sleeping wrist lay across mine. I studied the delicate contrast of her white wrist and the little pink and brown figures of cowboys on my pajamas. "Well? What do you say?" asked Gesh. I said I guessed so. We pulled on our corduroys, our white rubber boots, our mohair sweaters.

Downstairs the blood had begun to clot. In the hallway it was still sticky in places, but for the most part crusted dry. Outside a massive fibrinogenification was taking place under a dirt-brown sky. Scabs like thin coats of ice were forming over the deeper puddles; the mud was crusting underfoot; fresh blood ran off in streams and drainage ditches; the trees drooled clots of it in the hot breeze. "Wow! Dig that sky, bro—" Gesh said. "Brown as a turd."

"Yeah," I said, "it's weird. But thank Christ it stopped bleeding."

Gesh started the car while I broke the scab-crust from the

windshield: it flaked, and crumbled in dusty grains. I climbed in, laid some newspaper over the day-old vomit on the floor, steeled myself against the stench. Gesh accelerated in an attempt to back out from the wall: I could hear the wheels spinning. I poked my head out. We were stuck up to the frame in mud and gore. "Fuck it," Gesh said. "We'll take Scott's car." We started up the drive toward the other car. It was then that the first pasty lumps of it began to slap down sporadically; we reached the shelter of the porch just as it began to thunder down, heavy, feculent, and wet.

Upstairs we carefully folded our sweaters, pulled on our white pajamas, and sought out the warm spots in the huddled sleeping mass of us.

The Second Swimming

MAO FLICKS ON the radio. Music fills the room, half notes like the feet of birds. It is a martial tune, the prelude from "The Long March." Then there are quotations from Chairman Mao, read in a voice saturated with conviction, if a trifle nasal. A selection of the Chairman's poetry follows. The three constantly read articles. And then the aphorism for the hour. Mao sits back, the gelid features imperceptibly softening from their habitual expression of abdominal anguish. He closes his eyes.

FIGHTING LEPROSY WITH
REVOLUTIONARY OPTIMISM

Chang Chiu-chu of the Kunghui Commune found one day that the great toe of his left foot had become leprous. When the revisionist surgeons of the urban hospital insisted that they could not save the toe but only treat the

disease and hope to contain it, Chang went to Kao
Fei-fu, a revolutionary machinist of the commune. Kao
Fei-fu knew nothing of medicine but recalled to Chang
the Chairman's words: "IF YOU WANT KNOWL-
EDGE, YOU MUST TAKE PART IN THE PRAC-
TICE OF CHANGING REALITY. IF YOU WANT TO
KNOW THE TASTE OF A PEAR, YOU MUST
CHANGE THE PEAR BY EATING IT YOURSELF."
Kao then inserted needles in Chang's spinal column to a
depth of 18 fen. The following day Chang Chiu-chu was
able to return to the paddies. When he thanked Kao
Fei-fu, Kao said: "Don't thank me, thank Chairman
Mao."

Mao's face attempts a paternal grin, achieves the logy and
listless. Out in the square he can hear the planetary hum of
500,000 voices singing "The East Is Red." It is his birthday.
He will have wieners with Grey Poupon mustard for breakfast.

How he grins, Hung Ping-chung, hurrying through the
congested streets (bicycles, oxcarts, heads, collars, caps), a
brown-paper parcel under one arm, cardboard valise under
the other. In the brown-paper parcel, a pair of patched blue
jeans for his young wife, Wang Ya-chin. Haggled off the legs
of a Scandinavian tourist in Japan. For 90,000 yen. In the
cardboard valise, Hung's underwear, team jacket, paddle.
The table-tennis team has been on tour for thirteen months.
Hung thirsts for Wang.

There is a smear of mustard on Mao's nose when the barber
clicks through the bead curtains. The barber has shaved Mao
sixteen hundred and seven times. He bows, expatiates on the
dimension of the honor he feels in being of personal service to

the Revolutionary Chairman of the Chinese Communist Party. He then congratulates the Chairman on his birthday. "Long live Chairman Mao!" he shouts. "A long, long life to him!" Then he dabs the mustard from Mao's nose with a flick of his snowy towel.

Mao is seated in the lotus position, hands folded in his lap. Heavy of jowl, abdomen, nates. The barber strops.

"On the occasion of my birthday," says Mao, "I will look more like the Buddha." His voice is parched, riding through octaves like the creak of a rocking chair.

"The coiffure?"

Mao nods. "Bring the sides forward a hair, and take the top back another inch. And buff the pate."

Out on the Lei Feng Highway a cold rain has begun to fall. Chang Chiu-chu and his pig huddle in the lee of a towering monolithic sculpture depicting Mao's emergence from the cave at Yenan. Peasants struggle by, hauling carts laden with produce. Oxen bleat. A bus, the only motorized vehicle on the road, ticks up the hill in the distance. Chang's slippers are greasy with mud. He is on his way to the city to personally thank Mao for the healing of his great toe (the skin has gone from black to gray and sensation has begun to creep back like an assault of pinpricks) and to present the Chairman with his pig. There are six miles to go. His feet hurt. He is cold. But he recalls a phrase of the Chairman's: "I CARE NOT THAT THE WIND BLOWS AND THE WAVES BEAT: IT IS BETTER THAN IDLY STROLLING IN A COURTYARD," and he recalls also that he has a gourd of maotai (120 proof) in his sleeve. He pours a drink into his thermos-cup, mixes it with hot water and downs it. Then lifts a handful of cold rice from his satchel and begins to chew. He pours another drink. It warms his digestive machinery like a shot of Revolutionary Optimism.

Hung is two blocks from home, hurrying, the collar of his pajamas fastened against the cold, too preoccupied to wonder why he and his class brothers wear slippers and pajamas on the street rather than overshoes and overcoats. He passes under a poster: fierce-eyed women in caps and fatigues hurtling toward the left, bayonets and automatic weapons in hand. It is an advertisement for a ballet: "The Detachment of Red Women." Beneath it, a slogan, the characters big as washing machines, black on red: "GET IN THE HABIT OF NOT SPITTING ON THE GROUND AT RANDOM." The phlegm catches in his throat.

When Hung turns into his block, his mouth drops. The street has been painted red. The buildings are red, the front stoops are red, the railings are red, the lampposts are red, the windows are red, the pigeons are red. A monumental poster of Mao's head drapes the center of the block like an arras and clusters of smaller heads dot the buildings. Hung clutches the package to his chest, nods to old Chiung-hua where sh her stoop, a spot of gray on a carmine canvas, and t steps to his apartment two at a time.

Wang is in bed. The apartment is cold, dark. "Wang!" he shouts. "I'm back!" She does not rise to meet him, to leap into his arms in her aggressive elastic way (she a former tumbler, their romance a blossom of the People's Athletic and Revolutionary Fitness Academy). Something is wrong. "Wang!" She turns her black eyes to him and all at once he becomes aware of the impossible tumescence of the blanket spread over her. What is she concealing? She bites the corner of the blanket and groans, the labor pains coming fiercer now.

Hung is stung. Drops package and valise. Begins to count the months on his fingers. All thirteen of them. His face shrinks to the size of a pea. "Wang, what have you done?" he stammers.

Her voice is strained, unsteady: "YOU CAN'T SOLVE A

PROBLEM? WELL, GET DOWN AND INVESTIGATE
THE PRESENT FACTS AND ITS PAST HISTORY."
"You've been unfaithful!"
"Don't thank me," she croaks, "thank Chairman Mao."

Mao's eyes are closed. His cheeks glow, freshly shaven. In
his face, the soapy warm breath of the barber: in his ears, the
snip-snip of the barber's silver scissors. His shanks and seat
and the small of his back register the faint vibration of the
500,000 voices ringing in the square. A warmth, an electricity
tingling through the wood of the chair. Snip-snip.
Mao's dream is immediate and vivid. The sun breaking in
the east, sweet marjoram on the breeze, crickets singing along
the broad base of the Great Wall, a sound as of hidden fingers
working the blades of a thousand scissors. The times are
feudal. China is disunited, the Han Dynasty in decline, the
Huns (Hsiung-nu) demanding tribute of gold, spices, silk and
the soft, uncallused hands of the Emperor's daughters. They
wear impossible fierce mustaches stiffened with blood and
mucus, these Huns, and they keep the rain from their backs
with the stretched skin of murdered children. An unregener-
ate lot. Wallowing in the sins of revisionism and capitalist
avarice. Mao, a younger man, his brow shorter, eyes clearer,
jowls firmer, stands high atop the battlements supervising the
placement of the final stone. The Great Wall, he calls it,
thinking ahead to the Great Leap Forward and the Great Hall
of the People. Fifteen hundred miles long. Forty feet high,
sixteen across.
In the distance, a duststorm, a whirlwind, a thousand acres
of topsoil flung into the air by the terrible thundering hoofs of
the Huns' carnivorous horses. Their battle cry is an earth-
quake, their breath the death of a continent. On they come,
savage as steel, yabbering and howling over the clattering
cannonade of the horsehoofs while Mao's peasants pat the

mortar in place and quick-fry wonton in eighty-gallon drums of blistering oil. Mao stands above them all, the khaki collar visible beneath the red silk robe smoothing his thighs in the breeze. In his hand, held aloft, a Ping-Pong paddle.

The Huns rein their steeds. They are puzzled, their babble like the disquisitions of camels and jackals. From a breezy pocket Mao produces the eggshell-frail ball, sets it atop the paddle. The grizzled Hun-chief draws closer, just beneath the rippling Chairman. "Hua?" he shouts. Mao looks down. Cups his hands to his mouth: "Volley for serve."

Chang is having problems with his legs, feet. The left is reluctant to follow the right, and when it does, the right is reluctant to follow suit. To complicate matters the leprous toe has come to life (feeling very much like a fragment of glowing iron pounded flat on an anvil), and the pig has become increasingly insistent about making a wallow of the puddled road. A finger-thick brass ring pierces the pig's (tender) septum. This ring is fastened to a cord which is in turn fastened to Chang's belt. From time to time Chang gives the cord a tug, gentle persuader.

Ahead the buildings of the city cut into the bleak horizon like a gap-toothed mandible. The rain raises welts in the puddles, thrushes wing overhead, a man approaches on a bicycle. Chang pauses for a nip of maotai, as a sort of internal liniment for his throbbing toe, when suddenly the pig decides to sit, flip, flounder and knead the mud of the road with its rump. The cord jerks violently. Chang hydroplanes. Drops his gourd. Comes to rest in a dark puddle abob with what appears to be spittle randomly spat. He curses the animal's revisionist mentality.

There are two framed photographs on the wall over Wang's bed. One a full-face of Mao Tse-tung, the other a profile of

Liu Ping-pong, originator of table tennis. Hung tears the Mao from the wall and tramples it underfoot. Wang sings out her birthpangs. In the street, old Chiung-hua totters to her feet, listening. Her ancient ears, withered like dried apricots, tell her the first part of the story (the raised voice, slamming door, footsteps on the stairs), and the glassy eyes relay the rest (Hung in the crimson street, flailing at the gargantuan head of Mao suspended just above his reach like the proud stiff sail of a schooner; his use of stones, a broom, a young child; his frustration; his rabid red-mouthed dash down the length of the street and around the corner).

Chiung-hua sighs. Mao's head trembles in a gust. Wang cries out. And then the old woman hikes her skirts and begins the long painful ascent of the stairs, thinking of white towels and hot water and the slick red skulls of her own newborn sons and daughters, her spotted fingers uncertain on the banister, eyes clouding in the dark hallway, lips working over a phrase of Mao's like a litany: "WHAT WE NEED IS AN ENTHUSIASTIC BUT CALM STATE OF MIND AND IN-TENSE BUT ORDERLY WORK."

Mao is planted on one of the few toilet seats in China. The stall is wooden, fitted with support bars of polished bamboo. A fan rotates lazily overhead. An aide waits without. The Chairman is leaning to one side, penknife in hand, etching delicate Chinese characters into the woodwork. The hot odor that rises round him tells of aging organs and Grey Poupon mustard. He sits back to admire his work.

IMPERIALISM IS A PAPER TIGER

But then he leans forward again, the penknife working a refinement. The aide taps at the stall door. "Yes?" says Mao.

"Nothing," says the aide. Mao folds the blade back into its plastic sheath. The emendation pleases him.

IMPERIALISM SUCKS

The man lays his bicycle in the grass and reaches down a hand to help Chang from the mud. Chang begins to thank him, but the stranger holds up his hand. "Don't thank me," he says, "thank Chairman Mao." The stranger's breath steams in the chill air. He introduces himself. "Chou Te-ming." he says.

"Chang Chiu-chu."

"Chang Chiu-chu?"

Chang nods.

"Aren't you the peasant whose leukemia was cured through the application of Mao Tse-tung's thought?"

"Leprosy," says Chang, his toe smoldering like Vesuvius.

"I heard it on the radio," says Chou. "Two hundred times."

Chang beams. "See that pig?" he says. (Chou looks. The pig breaks wind.) "I'm on my way to the city to offer him up to the Chairman for his birthday. By way of thanks."

Chou, it seems, is also en route to the capital. He suggests that they travel together. Chang is delighted. Shakes the mud from his pantlegs, gives the pig's septum an admonitory tug, and then stops dead. He begins tapping his pockets.

"Lose something?" asks Chou.

"My gourd."

"Ah. Maotai?"

"Home-brewed. And sweet as rain."

The two drop their heads to scan the muddied roadway. Chang spots the gourd at the same moment the pig does, but the pig is lighter on its feet. Rubber nostril, yellow tusk: it snatches up the spotted rind and jerks back its head. The golden rice liquor drools like honey from the whiskered jowls. Snurk, snurk, snurk.

Old Chiung-hua lights the lamp, sets a pot of water on the stove, rummages through Wang's things in search of clean linen. Her feet ache and she totters with each step, slow and awkward as a hard-hat diver. Wang is quiet, her breathing regular. On the floor, in the center of the room, a brown-paper parcel. The old woman bends for it, then settles into a chair beside the bed. A Japanese-made transistor radio hangs from the bedpost on a leather strap. She turns it on.

ASSISTING MORE DEAF-MUTES TO SING "THE EAST IS RED"

It was raining, and the children of the Chanchai People's Revolutionary Rehabilitation Center could not go out of doors. The paraplegic children entertained themselves by repeating quotations of Mao Tse-tung and singing revolutionary songs of the Chairman's sayings set to music. But one of the deaf-mute children came to Chou Te-ming, a cadre of a Mao Tse-tung's thought propaganda team, in tears. She signed to him that it was her fondest wish to sing "The East Is Red" and to call out "Long live Chairman Mao, a long, long life to him!" with the others. While discussing the problem with some class brothers later that day, Chou Te-ming recalled a phrase of Chairman Mao's: "THE PRINCIPLE OF USING DIFFERENT METHODS TO RESOLVE DIFFERENT CONTRADICTIONS IS ONE WHICH MARXIST-LENINISTS MUST STRICTLY OB-SERVE." He was suddenly inspired to go to the children's dormitory and examine their Eustachian tubes and vocal apparatuses. He saw that in many cases the deaf-mute children's tubes were blocked and frenums ingrown. The next morning he operated. By that evening, eighteen of the twenty children were experiencing their fondest desire, singing "The East Is Red" in praise of Mao Tse-tung. This is a great victory of Mao Tse-tung's thought, a rich fruit of the Great Proletarian Revolution.

In the shifting shadows cast by the lamp, old Chiung-hua nods and Wang wakes with a cry on her lips.

When Mao steps out on the balcony the square erupts. Five hundred thousand voices in delirium. "Mao, Mao, Mao, Mao," they chant. Confetti flies, banners wave. Mammoth Mao portraits leap at the tips of upraised fingers. The Chairman opens his arms and the answering roar is like the birth of a planet. He looks down on the wash of heads and shoulders oscillating like the sea along a rocky shoreline, and he turns to one of his aides. "Tell me," he shouts, "did the Beatles ever have it this good?" The aide, an intelligent fellow, grins. Mao gazes back down at the crowd, his frozen jowls trembling with a rush of paternal solicitude. It is then that the idea takes him, then, on the balcony, on his birthday, the grateful joyous revolutionary proletarian class brothers and sisters surging beneath him and bursting spontaneously into song ("The East Wind Prevails Over the West Wind"). He cups a hand to the aide's ear. "Fetch my swimtrunks."

Though the table-tennis team has taken him to Japan, Malaysia, Albania, Zaire, Togoland and Botswana, Hung's mental horizons are not expansive. He is a very literal-minded fellow. When Wang made her announcement from between clenched teeth and dusky sheets, he did not pause to consider that "Thank Chairman Mao" has become little more than a catchword or that virgin births have been known to occur in certain regions and epochs and under certain conditions or even that some more prosaic progenitor may have turned the trick. But perhaps he didn't want to. Perhaps the shock cauterized some vital portion of the brain, some control center, and left him no vent but a species of mindless frothing rage. And what better object for such a rage than that ice-faced universal progenitor, that kindly ubiquitous father?

The pig is swimming on its feet, drunk, ears and testicles awash, eyes crossed, nostrils dripping. It has torn the cord free from Chang's pants and now trots an unsteady twenty paces ahead of Chang and Chou. Chou is walking his bicycle. Chang, rorschached in mud and none too steady of foot himself, limps along beside him. From time to time the two lengthen their stride in the hope of overtaking the pig, but the animal is both watchful and agile, and holds its liquor better than some.

They are by this time passing through the outskirts of the great city, winding through the ranks of shanties that cluster the hills like tumbled dominoes. The river, roiled and yellow, rushes on ahead of them. Chang is muttering curses under his breath. The pig's ears flap rhythmically. Overhead, somewhere in the thin bleak troposphere, the rain submits to a transubstantiation and begins to fall as snow. Chang flings a stone and the porker quickens its pace.

"But it's snowing—"
"Thirty degrees—"
"Your shingles—"
"Blood pressure—"
"Hemorrhoids—"

Mao waves them away, his aides, as if they were so many flies and mosquitoes. His face is set. Beneath the baggy khaki swimtrunks, his thin thick-veined legs, splayed feet. He slips into his slippers, pulls on a Mao tunic, and steps down the stairs, out the door and into the crowd.

They are still singing. Holding hands. Posters wave, banners flash, flakes fall. By the time Mao's presence becomes

known through the breadth of the crowd, he has already
mounted an elevated platform in the back of a truck. The roar
builds successively—from near to far—like mortar rounds in
the hills, and those closest to him press in on the truck,
ecstatic, frenzied, tears coursing down their cheeks, bowing
and beaming and genuflecting.

The truck's engine fires. Mao waves his cap. Thousands
pass out. And then the truck begins to inch forward, the
crowd parting gradually before it. Mao waves again. Mountains topple. Icebergs plunge into the sea. With the aid of an
aide he climbs still higher—to the seat of a chair mounted on
the platform—and raises his hand for silence. A hush falls over
the crowd: cheers choke in throats, tears gel on eyelashes,
squalling infants catch their breath. The clatter of the truck's
engine becomes audible, and then, for those fortunate
thousands packed against the fenders, Mao's voice. He is
saying something about the river. Three words, repeated over
and over. The crowd is puzzled. The Chairman's legs are
bare. There is a towel thrown over his shoulder. And then,
like the jolt of a radio dropped in bathwater, the intelligence
shoots through the crowd. They take up the chant. "To the
River! To the River!" The Chairman is going swimming.

Chang and Chou feel the tremor in the soles of their feet,
the blast on the wind. "They're cheering in the square," says
Chou. "Must be the celebration for Mao's birthday." The
trousers slap round his ankles as he steps up his pace. Chang
struggles to keep up, slowed by drink and toethrob, and by
his rube's sense of amaze at the city. Periodically he halts to
gape at the skyscrapers that rise from the bank of shanties
like pyramids stalking the desert, while people course by on
either side of him—peasants, workers, Red Guards, children—all rushing off to join in the rites. Ahead of him, the
back of Chou, doggedly pushing at the handlebars of his bicy-

cle, and far beyond Chou, just visible through the thicket of thighs and calves, the seductive coiled tail of the pig. "Wait!" he calls. Chou looks back over his shoulder: "Hurry!" There is another shout. And then another. The crowd is coming toward them!

Straight-backed and stiff-lipped, propped up by his aides, Mao rides the truckbed like a marble statue of himself, his hair and shoulders gone white with a fat-flake snow. The crowd is orderly ("THE MASSES ARE THE REAL HEROES," he is thinking), flowing out of the square and into the narrow streets with the viscous ease of lightweight oil. There is no shoving or toe-stamping. Those in front of the truck fan to the sides, remove their jackets and lay them over the white peach fuzz in the road. Then they kneel and bow their foreheads to the pavement while the black-grid tires grind over the khaki carpet. Light as milkweed, the snowflakes spin down and whiten their backs.

The sight of the river reanimates the Chairman. He lifts his arms like a conductor and the crowd rushes with hilarity and admiration. "Long live," etc., they cheer as he strips off his jacket to reveal the skinny-strap undershirt beneath, the swell of his belly. (At this shout, Hung, who is in the process of defacing a thirty-foot-high portrait of the Chairman in a tenement street three blocks away, pauses, puzzling. It is then that he becomes aware of the six teenagers in Mao shirts and red-starred caps. They march up to him in formation, silent, pure, austere and disciplined. Two of them restrain Hung's hands; the others beat him with their Mao-sticks, from scalp to sole, until his flesh takes on the color and consistency of a fermenting plum.) Mao steps down from the truck, his pudgy hand spread across an aide's shoulder, and starts jauntily off for the shoreline. People weep and laugh, applaud and cheer: a million fingers reach out to touch the Chairman's bare legs

and arms. As he reaches the water's edge they begin to dis-
robe, stripping to khaki shorts and panties and brassieres,
swelling hordes of them crowding the littoral, their clothes
mounting faster than the languid feathery snowflakes.

Two hundred yards up the shore Chou abandons his bike
along the roadway and dashes for the water, Chang hobbling
behind him, both neck-stretching to catch a glimpse of the
Chairman's entourage. Somewhere behind them a band begins to play and a loudspeaker cranks out a spate of Mao's
maxims. In the confusion, Chang finds himself unbuttoning
his shirt, loosing the string of his trousers, shucking the mud-
caked slippers. Chou already stands poised in the gelid muck,
stripped to shorts, waiting for Mao to enter the water. His
mouth is a black circle, his voice lost in the boom of the
crowd.

And then, miracle of miracles, Mao's ankles are submersed
in the yellow current, his calves, his knees! He pauses to slap
the icy water over his chest and shoulders—and then the
geriatric racing dive, the breaststroke, the square brow and
circular head riding smooth over the low-lapping waves! The
people go mad, Coney Island afire, and rush foaming into the
chill winter water—old women, children, expectant mothers,
thrilled by Mao's heroic example, charged by the passion to
share in the element which washes the Revolutionary Chairman of the Chinese Communist Party.

Chou is in, Chang hesitating on the bank, the snow blowing, his arms prickled with gooseflesh. The water foams like a
battle at sea. People fling themselves at the river shouting
praise of Chairman Mao. Chang shrugs and follows them.

The water is a knife. Colder than the frozen heart of the
universe. The current takes him, heaves him into a tangle of
stiffening limbs and shocked bodies, a mass of them clinging
together like worms in a can, the air splintering in his lungs,
the darkness below, a thousand hands, the mud, cold. He

does not catch a glimpse of the Chairman's entourage, nor does he have an opportunity to admire the clean stroke, the smooth glide of the Chairman's head over the storm-white waves, forging on.

Wang's features are dappled with sweat. Old Chiung-hua sips white tea and dabs at Wang's forehead with a handkerchief. "Push," she says. "Bear down and heave." At that moment, over the jabber of the radio and the clang of the pipes, a roar, as of numberless human voices raised in concert. Chiung-hua lifts her withered head and listens.

Suddenly the door pushes open. The old woman turns, expecting Hung. It is not Hung. It is a pig, black head, white shoulders, brass ring through the nose. "Shoo!" cries Chiung-hua, astonished. "Shoo!" The pig stares at her, then edges into the room apologetically. The old lady staggers angrily to her feet, but then Wang grabs her hand. Wang's teeth are gritted, her gymnast's muscles flexed. "Uh-oh," she says and Chiung-hua sits back down: a head has appeared between Wang's legs. "Push, push, push," the old woman hisses, and Wang obeys. There is a sound like a flushing toilet and then suddenly the infant is in Chiung-hua's wizened hands. She cuts the cord, dabs the blood and tissue from the puckered red face, and swaddles the tiny thing in the only clean clothes at hand: a pair of patched blue jeans.

Wang sits up and the old woman hands her the infant. She hefts it to look underneath. (A male. Heavy of jowl, abdomen, nates. And with hair on its head—the strangest growth of hair set across the most impossible expanse of brow. Square across.) Wang wrinkles her nose. "That smell," she says. "Like a barnyard."

Chiung-hua, remembering, turns to shoo the pig. But then her ancient face drops: the pig is kneeling.

Out in the street, so close it jars, a shout goes up.

Dada

W E WERE ORGANIZING the Second International Dada Fair. The first had been held fifty-seven years ago in Berlin. The second, we felt, was overdue. Friedrich had asked Jean Arp's grandson, Guillaume, to exhibit his *Static Hobbyhorse #2*, and Marcel Duchamp's daughter, Lise, had agreed to show her *Nude Descending Escalator*. All very well and fine. But we were stuck for a main attraction, a drawing card, the pièce de résistance. Then Werther came up with a suggestion that slapped us all with its brilliance: waves beat on the rocks, lights flashed in dark rooms. I remember it clearly. We were drinking imported beer in Klaus's loft, laying plans for the Fair. Werther slouched against a molded polyethylene reproduction of Tristan Tzara's *Upended Bicycle*, a silver paper knife beating a tattoo in his palm. Beside him, on the coffee table, lay a stack of magazines. Suddenly he jerked the knife to his lips, shouted "Dada Redivivus!" and thrust the blade into the slick cellulose heart of them. Then he stepped back. The knife had impaled a magazine in the center of the stack: we began to understand.

Werther extracted his prize and flipped back the page. It was a news magazine. Glossy cover. We gathered round. There, staring back at us, between the drum major's braided cap and the gold epaulettes, were the dark pinguid features of Dada made flesh: His Excellency Al Haji Field Marshal and President for Life of Uganda: Idi Amin Dada.

"Crazee!" said Friedrich, all but dancing.

"Epatant!" sang Klaus.

My name is Zoë. I grinned. We had our piece de résistance.

Two days later I flew into Entebbe via Pan African Airways. Big Daddy met me at the airport. I was wearing my thigh-high boots, striped culottes. His head was like a medicine ball. He embraced me, buried his nose in my hair. "I love Americans!" he said. Then he gave me a medal.

At the house in Kampala he stood among his twenty-two children like a sleepy brontosaur among the first tiny quick-blooded mammals. One of the children wore a white tutu and pink ribbons. "This one," he said, his hand on the child's head, "a girl." Then he held out his broad pink palm and panned across the yard where the rest of the brood rolled and leaped, pinched, climbed and burrowed like dark little insects. He grinned and asked me to marry him. I was cagey. "After the Fair," I said.

"The Fair," he repeated. His eyes were sliced melons.

"Dada," I said.

The plane was part of a convoy of three Ugandan 747's. All across Zaire, Cameroon and Mali, across Mauritania and the rocky Atlantic, my ears sang with the keen of infants, the cluck of chickens, the stringy flatulence of goats and pigs. I looked out the window: the wing was streaked with rust. To the right and left, fore and aft, Big Daddy's bodyguards reclined in their reclining seats, limp as cooked spaghetti. High-heeled boots, shades and wristwatches, guns. Each held a transistor radio to his ear. Big Daddy sat beside me, sweating, caressing my fingers in a hand like a boxing glove. I was wearing two hundred necklaces and a turban. I am twenty-six. My hair is white, shag-cut. He was wearing a jumbo jumpsuit, khaki and camouflage, a stiff chest full of medals. I began to laugh.

"Why you laugh?" he said.

I was thinking of Bergson. I explained to him that the comical consists of something mechanical encrusted on the living. He stared at me, blank, his face misshapen as a decaying jack-o'-lantern.

"Dada," I said, by way of shorthand explication.

He grinned. Lit a cigarette. "They do me honor," he said finally, "to name such a movement for me."

The Fair was already under way when we landed at Kennedy. Big Daddy's wives, cattle and attendants boarded five rented buses and headed for Harlem, where he had reserved the fourth floor of the Hotel Theresa. His Excellency himself made a forty-five-minute impromptu speech at Gate 19E, touching on solutions to the energy crisis, inflation and overcrowded zoos, after which I hustled him into a cab and made for Klaus's loft on Elizabeth Street.

We rattled up Park Avenue, dipping and jolting, lights raining past the windows. Big Daddy told me of his athletic and military prowess, nuzzled my ear, pinned a medal to my breast. "Two hundred cattle," he said. "A thousand acre." I looked straight ahead. He patted my hand. "Twenty

bondmaids, a mountain of emeralds, fresh fish three days a
week."

I turned to look into the shifting deeps of his eyes, the lights
filming his face, yellow, green, red, bright, dark. "After the
Fair," I said.

The street outside Klaus's was thronged, the hallway
choked. The haut monde emerged from taxis and limousines
in black tie and jacket, Halston, Saint-Laurent, mink. "Fantastic!" I said. Big D. looked baleful. "What your people need
in this country is savannah and hippo," he said. "But your
palace very fine."

I knotted a gold brocade DADA sign around his neck and
led him up the stairs to a burst of applause from the spec-
tators. Friedrich met us at the door. He'd arranged everything. Duchamp's *Urinal* stood in the corner; DeGroff's soiled
diapers decorated the walls; Werther's own *Soir de l'Uganda*
dominated the second floor. Big Daddy squeezed my hand,
beamed like a tame Kong. There were champagne, canapés,
espresso, women with bare backs. A man was strapped to a
bicycle suspended from the ceiling.

Friedrich pumped Big Daddy's hand and then showed him
to the seat prepared for him as part of the *Soir de l'Uganda*
exhibit. It was magnificent. A thousand and one copper tulips
against a backdrop of severed heads and crocodiles. Big D.
affixed a medal to Friedrich's sweatshirt and settled into his
seat with a glass of champagne. Then he began his "People
Must Love Their Leaders" speech.

A reporter took me by the arm and asked me to explain the
controlling concept of the Fair and of our principal exhibit. It
was a textbook question. I gave him a textbook answer. "Any
object is a work of art if the artist proclaims it one," I said.
"There is static, cerebral art and there is living art, monuments of absurdity—acts of art. And actors." Then he asked

me if it was true that I had agreed to become Big Daddy's fifth wife. The question surprised me. I looked over at the *Soir de l'Uganda* exhibit. Two of the bodyguards were shooting craps against the bank of papier-mâché heads. Big Daddy slouched in his chair, elephantine and black, beleaguered by lords and ladies, photographers, reporters, envious artists. I could hear his voice over the natter of the crowd—a basso profundo that crept into the blood and punched at the kidneys. "I am a pure son of Africa," he was saying. Overhead the bicycle wheels whirred. I turned back to the reporter, an idea forming in my head—an idea so outré that it shot out to scrape at the black heart of the universe. The ultimate act of art. Dada sacrifice!

He stood there, pen poised over the paper.

"Da," I said. "Da."

A Women's Restaurant

> . . . the monomaniac incarnation
> of all those malicious agencies
> which some deep men feel eating
> in them, till they are left living on
> with half a heart and half a lung.

> —Melville, *Moby Dick*

I

IT IS A WOMEN'S RESTAURANT. Men are not permitted.
Women go there to be in the company of other women, to
sit in the tasteful rooms beneath the ancient revolving fans
and the cool green of spilling plants, to cross or uncross their
legs as they like, to chat, sip liqueurs, eat. At the door, the first
time they enter, they are asked to donate twenty-five cents

and they are issued a lifetime membership card. Thus the
women's restaurant has the legal appearance of a private club,
and its proprietors, Grace and Rubie, avoid running afoul of
the antidiscrimination laws. A women's restaurant. What goes
on there, precisely, no man knows. I am a man. I am burning
to find out.

This I do know: they drink wine. I have been out back, at
night, walking my dog, and I have seen the discarded bottles:
chablis, liebfraumilch, claret, mountain burgundy, Bristol
Cream. They eat well too. The garbage is rich with dark exotic
coffee grounds and spiced teas, the heads of sole, leaves of
artichoke, shells of oyster. There is correspondence in the
trash as well. Business things for the most part, but once there
was a letter from Grace's mother in Moscow, Iowa. Some of
the women smoke cigars. Others—perhaps the same ones—
drive motorcycles. I watched two of them stutter up on a
Triumph 750. In leathers. They walked like meat-packers,
heavy, shoulders back, hips tight. Up the steps of the front
porch, through the curtained double doors, and in. The doors
closed like eyes in mascara.

There is more. Grace, for instance. I know Grace. She is
tall, six three or four I would guess, thin and slightly stooped,
her shoulders rounded like a question mark. Midthirties. Not
married. She walks her square-headed cat on a leash, an ad-
vocate of women's rights. Rubie I have spoken with. If Grace
is austere, a cactus tall and thorny, Rubie is lush, a spreading
peony. She is a dancer. Five feet tall, ninety pounds,
twenty-four years old. Facts. She told me one afternoon,
months ago, in a bar. I was sitting at a table, alone, reading, a
glass of beer sizzling in the sunlight through the window. Her
arms and shoulders were bare, the thin straps of her dancer's
tights, blue jeans. She was twirling, on points, between
groups of people, her laughter like a honky-tonk piano. She

came up from behind, ran her finger along the length of my nose, called it elegant. Her own nose was a pug nose. We talked. She struck poses, spoke of her body and the rigors of dancing, showed me the hard muscle of her arms. The sun slanted through the high windows and lit her hair. She did not ask about my life, about the book I was reading, about how I make a living. She did not sit down. When she swept away in a series of glissades, her arms poised, I ordered another beer. She wouldn't know me on the street.

The women's restaurant fronts a street that must have been a main thoroughfare fifty years ago. It comprises the whole of an old mansion, newly painted and shuttered. There is a fence, a gate, a tree, a patch of lawn. Gargoyles. The mayor may once have lived there. On either side blocks of two-story brick buildings stretch to the street corners like ridges of glacial detritus. Apartments above, storefronts below: a used clothing store, an organic merchant, a candle shop. Across the street, incongruous, is a bar that features a picture window and topless dancers. From behind this window, washed in shadow, I reconnoiter the women's restaurant.

I have watched women of every stripe pass through those curtained front doors: washerwomen, schoolmarms, gymnasts, waitresses, Avon ladies, scout leaders, meter maids, grandmothers, great-grandmothers, spinsters, widows, dikes, gay divorcées, the fat, the lean, the wrinkled, the bald, the sagging, the firm, women in uniform, women in scarves and bib overalls, women in stockings, skirts and furs, the towering Grace, the flowing Rubie, a nun, a girl with a plastic leg— and yes, even the topless dancers. There is something disturbing about this gathering of women, this classless convocation, this gynecomorphous melting pot. I think of Lysistrata, Gertrude Stein, Carry Nation.

My eyes and ears are open. Still, what I have come to know
of Grace & Rubie's is what any interested observer might
know. I hunger for an initiate's knowledge.

II

I have made my first attempt to crack the women's restaurant.

The attempt was repulsed.

I was sitting at the picture window of the topless bar,
chain-drinking tequila and tonic, watching the front porch of
Grace & Rubie's, the bloom of potted flowers, the promise of
the curtained doors, and women, schools of them, electric
with color, slamming car doors, dismounting from bicycles,
motorcycles, trotting up the steps, in and out, tropical fish
behind a spotted pane of glass. The sun was drifting toward
the horizon, dipping behind the twin chimneys, spooning
honey over the roof, the soft light blurring edges and corners,
smoothing back the sneers of the gargoyles. It was then that I
spotted Rubie. Her walk fluid and unperturbed as a drifting
skater. There was another girl with her, an oriental girl. Black
hair like a coat. I watched the door gape and then swallow
them. Then I stood, put some money in my pocket, left some
on the table, and stepped out into the street.

It was warm. The tree was budding. The sun had dropped a
notch and the house flooded the street with shadow. I swam
toward it, blood beating quick, stopped at the gate to look
both ways, pushed through and mounted the steps. Then
made my first mistake. I knocked. Knocked. Who knocks at
the door of a restaurant? No one answered. I could hear music
through the door. Electric jazz. I peered through the oval
windows set in the door and saw that the curtains were very
thick indeed. I felt uneasy. Knocked again.

After an interval Grace opened the door. Her expression was puzzled. "Yes?" she said.

I was looking beyond her, feeling the pulse of the music, aware of a certain indistinct movement in the background, concentrating on the colors, plants, polished woodwork. Underwater. Chagall.

"Can I help you?"

"Yes, you can," I said. "I'd like—ah—a cup of coffee for starters, and I'd like to see the menu. And your wine list."

"I'm very sorry," Grace said. "But this is a women's restaurant."

III

A women's restaurant. The concept inflames me. There are times, at home, fish poached, pots scrubbed, my mind gone blank, when suddenly it begins to rise in my consciousness, a sunken log heaving to the surface. A women's restaurant. The injustice of it, the snobbery, the savory dark mothering mystery: what do they *do* in there?

I picture them, Rubie, Grace, the oriental girl, the nun, the girl with one leg, all of them—picture them sipping, slouching, dandling sandals from their great toes (a mental peep beneath the skirts). I see them dropping the coils of their hair, unfastening their brassieres, rubbing the makeup from their faces. They are soft, heavy, glowing with muliebrity. The pregnant ones remove their tentish blouses, pinching shoes, slacks, underwear, and begin a slow primitive shuffle to the African beat of the drums and the cold moon music of the electric piano. The others watch, chanting, an arcane language, a formula, locked in a rhythm and a mystery that soar grinning above all things male, dark and fertile as the earth.

Or perhaps they're shooting pool in the paneled back room,

cigars smoking, brandy in snifters, eyes intense, their breasts pulled toward the earth, the slick cue sticks easing through the dark arches of their fingers, stuffed birds on the walls, the glossy balls clacking, riding down the black pockets like burrowing things darting for holes in the ground . . .

IV

Last night there was a fog, milk in an atomizer. The streets steamed. Turner, I thought. Fellini. Jack the Ripper. The dog led me to the fence outside the women's restaurant, where he paused to sniff and balance on three legs. The house was a bank of shadow, dark in a negligee of moonlit mist. Fascinating, enigmatic, compelling as a white whale. Grace's VW hunched at the curb behind me, the moon sat over the peaked roof cold as a stone, my finger was on the gate. The gate was latched. I walked on, then walked back. Tied the dog to one of the pickets, reached through to unlatch the gate, and stepped into the front yard at Grace & Rubie's for the second time.

This time I did not knock.

Instead I slipped up to a window and peered through a crack in the curtains. It was black as the inside of a closet. On an impulse I tried the window. It was locked. At that moment a car turned into the street, tires chirping, engine revving, the headlights like hounds of heaven. Rubie's Fiat.

I lost my head. Ran for the gate, tripped, scrambled back toward the house, frantic, ashamed, mortified. Trapped. The car hissed to a stop, the engine sang a hysterical chorus, the headlights died. I heard voices, the swat of car doors. Keys rattling. I crouched. Then crept into the shrubbery beneath the porch. Out by the fence the dog began to whimper.

Heels. Muffled voices. Then Rubie: "Aww, a puppy. And what's he doing out here, huh?" This apparently addressed to the dog, whose whimpering cut a new octave. I could hear his tail slapping the fence. Then a man's voice, impatient. The gate creaked, slapped shut. Footsteps came up the walk. Stopped at the porch. Rubie giggled. Then there was silence. My hand was bleeding. I was stretched out prone, staring at the ground. They were kissing. "Hey," said Rubie, soft as fur, "I like your nose—did I tell you that?"

"How about letting me in tonight," he whispered. "Just this once."

Silence again. The rustle of clothing. I could have reached out and shined their shoes. The dog whimpered.

"The poor pup," Rubie breathed.

"Come on," the guy said. I hated him.

And then, so low I could barely catch it, like a sleeping breath or the hum of a moth's wing: "Okay." Okay? I was outraged. This faceless cicisbeo, this panting lover, schmuck, male—this shithead was going to walk into Grace & Rubie's just like that? A kiss and a promise? I wanted to shout out, call the police, stop this unthinkable sacrilege.

Rubie's key turned in the lock. I could hear the shithead's anticipatory breathing. A wave of disillusion deadened me. And then suddenly the porch light was blazing, bright as a cafeteria. I shrank. Grace's voice was angry. "What is this?" she hissed. I held my breath.

"Look—" said Rubie.

"No men allowed," said Grace. "None. Ever. Not now, not tomorrow—you know how I feel about this sort of thing."

"—Look, I pay rent here too—"

I could hear the shithead shuffling his feet on the dry planks of the porch. Then Grace: "I'm sorry. You'll have to leave." In the shadows, the ground damp, my hand bleeding, I began to smile.

The door slammed. Someone had gone in. Then I heard Grace's voice swelling to hurricane pitch, and Rubie raging back at her like a typhoon. Inside. Muffled by the double

doors, oval windows, thick taffeta curtains. The shithead's feet
continued to shuffle on the porch. A moment ticked by, the
voices storming inside, and then the light cut out. Dead.
Black. Night.

My ears followed the solitary footsteps down the walk,
through the gate and into the street.

V

I shadowed Rubie for eight blocks this morning. There
were packages in her arms. Her walk was the walk of a slow-
haunching beast. As she passed the dark windows of the shops
she turned to watch her reflection, gliding, flashing in the
sun, her bare arms, clogs, the tips of her painted toenails
peeping from beneath the wide-bottomed jeans. Her hair
loose, undulating across her back like a wheatfield in the
wind. She stopped under the candy-striped pole outside
Red's Barber Shop.

I crossed the street, sat on a bench and opened a book.
Then I saw Grace: slouching, wide-striding, awkward. Her
sharp nose, the bulb of frizzed hair. She walked up to Rubie,
unsmiling. They exchanged cheek-pecks and stepped into the
barber shop.

When they emerged I dropped my book: Rubie was dese-
crated. Her head shaven, the wild lanks of hair hacked to
stubble. Charley Manson, I thought. Auschwitz. Nuns and
neophytes. Grace was smiling. Rubie's ears stuck out from her
head, the color of butchered chicken. Her neck and temples
were white as flour, blue-veined and vulnerable. I was appalled.

They walked quickly, stiffly, Rubie hurrying to match
Grace's long strides. Grace a sunflower, Rubie a stripped
dandelion. I followed them to the women's restaurant. Rubie
did not turn to glance at her reflection in the shop windows.

VI

I have made my second attempt to crack the women's restaurant.

The attempt was repulsed.

This time I was not drunk: I was angry. Rubie's desecration had been rankling me all day. While I could approve of Grace's firmness with the faceless cicisbeo, I could not countenance her severity toward Rubie. She is like a stroke of winter, I thought, folding up Rubie's petals, traumatizing her roots. An early frost, a blight. But then I am neither poet nor psychologist. My metaphors are primitive, my actions impulsive.

I kicked the gate open, stamped up the front steps, twisted the doorknob and stepped into the women's restaurant. My intentions were not clear. I thought vaguely of rescuing Rubie, of entering that bastion of womanhood, of sex and mystery and rigor, and of walking out with her on my arm. But I was stunned. Frozen. Suddenly, and after all those weeks, I had done it. I was inside.

The entrance hall was narrow and dark, candlelit, over-heated, the walls shaggy with fern and wandering Jew. Music throbbed like blood. I felt squeezed, pinched, confined, Buster Crabbe in the shrinking room. My heart left me. I was slouching. Ahead, at the far end of the hallway, a large room flowered in darkness and lights glowed red. Drum, drum, drum, the music like footsteps. That dim and deep central chamber drawing me: a women's restaurant, a women's restaurant: the phrase chanted in my head.

And then the door opened behind me. I turned. Two of the biker girls stepped through the doorway, crowding the hall. One of them was wearing a studded denim jacket, the collar turned up. Both were tall. Short-haired. Their shoulders congested the narrow hallway. I wheeled and started for the darkened room ahead. But stopped in midstride. Grace was there, a tray in her hand, her face looking freshly slapped. "You!" she hissed. The tray fell, glasses shattered, I was grabbed from behind. Rabbit-punched. One of the biker girls began emitting fierce gasping oriental sounds as her white fists and sneakered feet lashed out at me. I went down, thought I saw Rubie standing behind Grace, a soft flush of alarm suffusing her cheeks. A rhythm developed. The biker girls kicked, I huddled. Then they had me by belt and collar, the door was flung open and they rocked me, one, two, three, the bum's rush, down the front steps and onto the walk. The door slammed.

I lay there for a moment, hurting. Then I became aware of the clack of heels on the pavement. A woman was coming up the walk: skirt, stockings, platforms. She hesitated when she saw me there. And then, a look of disgust creasing her makeup, she stepped over me as if she were stepping over a worm or a fat greasy slug washed up in a storm. Her perfume was devastating.

VII

I have been meditating on the essential differences between men and women, isolating distinguishing traits. The meditation began with points of dissimilarity. Women, I reasoned, do not have beards, while they do have breasts. And yet I have seen women with beards and men with breasts—in fact, I came to realize, all men have breasts. Nipples too. Ah, but women have long hair, I thought. Narrow shoulders, expansive hips. Five toes on each foot. Pairs of eyes, legs, arms, ears. But ditto men. They are soft, yielding, dainty, their sensibilities refined—they like shopping. I ran through all the stereotypes, dismissed them one after another. There was only one distinguishing sexual characteristic, I concluded. A hole. A hole as dark and strange, as fascinating and forbidding, as that interdicted entrance to Grace & Rubie's. Birth and motherhood, I thought. The maw of mystery.

I have also been perusing a letter from Rubie, addressed to a person named Jack. The letter is a reconstruction of thirty-two fragments unearthed in the trash behind the women's restaurant. "I miss you and I love you, Jack," the letter said in part, "but I cannot continue seeing you. My responsibilities are here. Yes I remember the night on the beach, the night in the park, the night at the cabin, the night on the train, the night in Saint Patrick's Cathedral—memories I will always cherish. But it's over. I am here. A gulf separates us. I owe it to Grace. Take care of yourself and your knockout nose. Love, R." The letter disturbs me. In the same way that the women's restaurant disturbs me. Secrets, stifling secrets. I want admission to them all.

VIII

The girl in the department store asked me what size my wife took. I hesitated. "She's a big one," I said. "About the same size as me." The girl helped me pick out a pink polyester pantsuit, matching brassiere, tall-girl panty hose. Before leaving the store I also visited the ladies' shoe department and the cosmetic counter. At the cosmetic counter I read from a list: glosser, blusher, hi-lighter, eyeshadow (crème, cake and stick), mascara, eyeliner, translucent powder, nail polish (frosted pink), spike eyelashes, luscious tangerine lipstick, tweezers, a bottle of My Sin and the current issue of *Be Beautiful*. At the shoe department I asked for Queen Size.

IX

After two weeks of laying foundation, brushing on, rubbing in, tissuing off, my face was passable. Crude, yes—like the slick masks of the topless dancers—but passable nonetheless. And my hair, set in rollers and combed out in a shoulder-length flip, struck close on the heels of fashion. I was no beauty, but neither was I a dog.

I eased through the gate, sashayed up the walk, getting into the rhythm of it. Bracelets chimed at my wrists, rings shot light from my fingers. Up the steps, through the front door and into that claustrophobic hallway. My movement fluid, silky, the T-strap flats gliding under my feet like wind on water. I was onstage, opening night, and fired for the performance. But then I had a shock. One of the biker girls slouched at the end of the hallway lighting a cigar. I tossed my chin and strutted by. Our shoulders brushed. She grinned. "Hi," she breathed. I stepped past her, and into the forbidden room.

It was dark. Candlelit. There were tables, booths, sofas and lounge chairs. Plants, hangings, carpets, woodwork. Women. I held back. Then felt a hand on my elbow. It was the biker. "Can I buy you a drink?" she said.

I shook my head, wondering what to do with my voice. Falsetto? A husky whisper?

"Come on," she said. "Get loose. You're new here, right? —you need somebody to show you around." She pinched my elbow and ushered me to a booth across the room—wooden benches like church pews. I slid in, she eased down beside me. I could feel her thigh against mine. "Listen," I said, opting for the husky whisper, "I'd really rather be alone—"

Suddenly Rubie was standing over us. "Would you like something?" she said.

The biker ordered a Jack Daniel's on the rocks. I wanted a beer, asked for a sunrise. "Menu?" said Rubie. She was wearing a leather apron, and she seemed slimmer, her shoulders rounded. Whipped, I thought. Her ears protruded and her brushcut bristled. She looked like a cub scout. An Oliver Twist.

"Please," I said, huskily.

She looked at me. "Is this your first time?"

I nodded.

She dug something—a lavender card—from an apron pocket. "This is our membership card. It's twenty-five cents for a lifetime membership. Shall I put it on the bill?"

I nodded. And followed her with my eyes as she padded off. The biker turned to me. "Ann Jenks," she said, holding out her hand.

I froze. A name, a name, a name. This part I hadn't considered. I pretended to study the menu. The biker's hand hung in the air. "Ann Jenks," she repeated.

"Valerie," I whispered, and nearly shook hands. Instead I held out two fingers, ladylike. She pinched them, rubbed her thumb over the knuckles and looked into my eyes.

Then Rubie appeared with our drinks. "Cheers," said Ann Jenks. I downed the libation like honey and water.

An hour and a half later I was two sheets to the wind and getting cocky. Here I was, embosomed in the very nave, the very omphalos of furtive femininity—a prize patron of the women's restaurant, a member, privy to its innermost secrets. I sipped at my drink, taking it all in. There they were—women—chewing, drinking, digesting, chatting, giggling, crossing and uncrossing their legs. Shoes off, feet up. Smoking cigarettes, flashing silverware, tapping time to the music. Women among women. I bathed in their soft chatter, birdsong, the laughter like falling coils of hair. I lit a cigarette, and grinned. No more fairybook-hero thoughts of rescuing Rubie—oh no, this was paradise.

Below the table, in the dark, Ann Jenks's fingertips massaged my knee.

I studied her face as she talked (she was droning on about awakened consciousness, liberation from the mores of straight society, feminist terrorism). Her cheekbones were set high and cratered the cheeks below, the hair lay flat across her crown and rushed straight back over her ears, like duck's wings. Her eyes were black, the mouth small and raw. I snubbed out the cigarette, slipped my hand under the jacket and squeezed her breast. Then I put my tongue in her mouth.

"Hey," she said, "want to go?"

I asked her to get me one more drink. When she got up I slid out and looked for the restroom. It was a minor emergency: six tequila sunrises and a carafe of dinner wine tearing at my vitals. I fought an impulse to squeeze my organ.

There were plants everywhere. And behind the plants, women. I passed the oriental girl and two housewives/divorcées in a booth, a nun on a divan, a white-haired woman and her daughter. Then I spotted the one-legged girl, bump and grind, passing through a door adjacent to the kitchen. I followed.

The restroom was pink, carpeted: imitation marble countertops, floodlit mirrors, three stalls. Grace was emerging from the middle one as I stepped through the door. She smiled at me. I smiled back, sweetly, my bladder aflame. Then rushed into the stall, fought down the side zipper, tore at the silky panties, and forgot to sit down. I pissed, long and hard. Drunk. Studying the graffiti—women's graffiti. I laughed, flushed, turned to leave. But there was a problem: a head suspended over the door to the stall. Angry eyes. The towering Grace.

I shrugged my shoulders and held out my palms. Grace's face was the face of an Aztec executioner. This time there would be no quarter. I felt sick. And then suddenly my shoulder hit the door like a wrecker's ball, Grace sat in the sink, and the one-legged girl began gibbering from the adjoining compartment. Out the door and into the kitchen, rushing down an aisle lined with ovens, the stink of cooking food, scraps, greased-over plates, a screen door at the far end, slipping in the T-straps, my brassiere working round, Grace's murderous rasping shriek at my back, STOP HIM! STOP HIM!, and Rubie, pixie Rubie, a sack of garbage in her hand at the door.

Time stopped. I looked into Rubie's eyes, imploring, my breath cut in gasps, five feet from her. She let the garbage fall. Then dropped her head and right shoulder, and hit my knees like a linebacker. I went down. My face in coffee grounds and eggshells. Rubie's white white arms shackles on my legs and on my will.

X

I have penetrated the women's restaurant, yes, but in actuality it was little more than a rape. There was no sympathy, I did not belong: why kid myself? True, I do have a lifetime membership card, and I was—for a few hours at any rate—an unexceptionable patron of the women's restaurant. But that's not enough. I am not satisfied. The obsession grows in me, pregnant, swelling, insatiable with the first taste of fulfillment. Before I am through I will drink it to satiety. I have plans.

Currently, however, I am unable to make bail. Criminal trespass (Rubie testified that I was there to rob them, which, in its way is true I suppose), and assault (Grace showed the bruises on her shins and voice box where the stall door had hit her). Probation I figure. A fine perhaps. Maybe even psychiatric evaluation.

The police have been uncooperative, antagonistic even.

Malicious jokes, pranks, taunts, their sweating red faces fastened to the bars night and day. There has even been brutality. Oddly enough—perhaps as a reaction to their jibes—I have come to feel secure in these clothes. I was offered shirt, pants, socks, shoes, and I refused them. Of course, these things are getting somewhat gritty, my makeup is a fright, and my hair has lost its curl. And yet I defy them.

In drag. I like the sound of it. I like the feel. And, as I say, I have plans. The next time I walk through those curtained doors at Grace & Rubie's there will be no dissimulation. I will stroll in and I will belong, an initiate, and I will sit back and absorb the mystery of it, feed on honeydew and drink the milk of paradise. There are surgeons who can assure it.

After all, it is a women's restaurant.

The Extinction Tales

> I will show you fear in a handful of dust.
>
> —T. S. Eliot, *The Waste Land*

HE WAS IN his early fifties, between jobs, his wife dead ten years. When he saw the position advertised in the Wellington paper it struck him as highly romantic, and he was immediately attracted to it.

LIGHTHOUSEKEEPER. Stephen Island. References. Inquire T. H. Penn, Maritime Authority.

He took it. Sold his furniture, paid the last of the rent, filled two duffel bags with socks and sweaters and his bird watcher's guide, and hired a cart. Just as he was leaving, a neighbor approached him with something in her arms: pointed ears,

yellow eyes. Take it, she said. For company. He slipped the
kitten into the breast of his pea coat, waved, and started off
down the road.

Stephen Island is an eruption of sparsely wooded rock seventeen miles northwest of Wellington. It is uninhabited. At
night the constellations wheel over its quarter-mile radius like
mythical beasts.

The man was to be relieved for two weeks every six months.
He planted a garden, read, fished, smoked by the sea. The cat
grew to adolescence. One afternoon it came to him with a
peculiar bird clenched in its teeth. The man took the bird
away, puzzled over it, and finally sent it to the national
museum at Wellington for identification. Three weeks later a
reply came. He had discovered a new species: the Stephen
Island wren. In the interim the cat had brought him fourteen
more specimens of the odd little buff and white bird. The man
never saw one of the birds alive. After a while the cat stopped
bringing them.

In 1945, when the Russians liberated Auschwitz, they
found 129 ovens in the crematorium. The ovens were six
feet long, two feet high, one and a half feet wide.

The Union Pacific Railroad had connected New York,
Chicago and San Francisco, Ulysses S. Grant was stamping
about the White House in high-top boots, Jay Gould was
buying up gold, and Jared Pink was opening a butcher shop in
downtown Chicago.

PINK'S POULTRY, BEEF AND GAME

The town was booming. Barouches and cabriolets at every
corner, men in beavers and frock coats lining the steps of the

private clubs, women in bustles, bonnets and flounces giving teas and taking boxes at the theater. Thirty-room mansions, friezes, spires, gargoyles, the opera house, the exchange, shops, saloons, tenements. In the hardpan streets men and boys trailed back from the factories, stockyards, docks, their faces mapped in sweat and soot and the blood of animals.

All of them ate meat. Pink provided it. Longhorns from Texas, buffalo from the plains, deer, turkey, pheasant and pigeon from Michigan and Illinois. They stormed his shop, the bell over the door rushing and trilling as they bought up everything he could offer them, right down to the scraps in the brine barrels. Each day he sold out his stock and in the morning found himself at the mercy of his suppliers. A pre-dawn trip to the slaughterhouse for great swinging sides of beef, livers and tripe, blood for pudding, intestine for sausage. And then twice a week to meet the Michigan Line and the long low boxcars strung with dressed deer and piled deep with pigeons stinking of death and excrement. Unplucked, their feathers a nightmare, they filled the cars four feet deep and he would bring a boy along to shovel them into his wagon. They sold like a dream.

When his supplier tripled the price per bird Pink sent his brother Seth up to the nesting grounds near Petoskey, Michigan. As Seth's train approached Petoskey the sky began to darken. He checked his pocket watch: it was three in the afternoon. He leaned over the man beside him to look out the window. The sky was choked with birds, their mass blotting the sun, the drone of their wings and dry rattling feathers audible over the chuff of the engine. Seth whistled. Are those—? he said. Yep, said the man. Passenger pigeons.

Seth wired his brother from the Petoskey station. Two days later he and Jared were stalking the nesting grounds with a pair of Smith & Wesson shotguns and a burlap sack. They were not alone. The grove was thronged with hunters, hundreds of them, drinking, shooting, springing traps and tossing nets. Retrievers barked, shotguns boomed. At the far edge of the field women sat beneath parasols with picnic lunches.

Jared stopped to watch an old man assail the crown of a big-boled chestnut with repeated blasts from a brace of shotguns. A grim old woman stood at the man's elbow, reloading, while two teenagers scrambled over the lower branches of the tree, dropping nestlings to the ground. Another man, surrounded by dirt-faced children, ignited a stick of dynamite and pitched it into a tree thick with roosting birds. A breeze ruffled the leaves as the spitting cylinder twisted through them, pigeons cooing and clucking in the shadows—then there was a flash, and a concussion that thundered over the popping of shotguns from various corners of the field. Heads turned. The smoke blew off in a clot. Feathers, twigs, bits of leaf and a fine red mist began to settle. The children were already beneath the tree, on their hands and knees, snatching up the pigeons and squab as they fell to earth like ripe fruit.

Overhead the sky was stormy with displaced birds. Jared fired one barrel, then the other. Five birds slapped down, two of them stunned and hopping. He rushed them, flailing with the stock of his gun until they lay still. He heard Seth fire behind him. The flock was the sky, shrieking and reeling, panicked, the chalky white excrement like a snowstorm. Jared's hair and shoulders were thick with it, white spots flecked his face. He was reloading. There's got to be a better way, he said.

Three weeks later he and his brother returned to Petoskey. They rode out to the nesting grounds in a horse-drawn wagon, towing an old Civil War cannon behind them. In the bed of the wagon lay a weighted hemp net, one hundred feet square, and a pair of cudgels. Strips of cotton broadcloth had been sewed into the center of the net to catch the wind and insure an even descent, but the net fouled on its maiden flight and Seth had to climb a silver maple alive with crepitating pigeons to retrieve it. They refolded the net, stuffed it into the mouth of the cannon, and tried again. This time they were successful: Seth flushed the birds from the tree with a shotgun blast, the cannon roared, and Jared's net caught them as they rose. Nearly two thousand pigeons lay tangled in the mesh, their distress calls echoing through the trees, metallic and forlorn. The two brothers stalked over the grounded net with their cudgels, crushing the heads of the survivors. When the net had ceased to move and the blood had begun to settle into abstract patterns in the broadcloth, they dropped their cudgels and embraced, hooting and laughing like prospectors on a strike. We'll be rich! Seth shouted.

He was right. Within six months PINK'S POULTRY, BEEF AND GAME was turning over as many as seventeen thousand pigeons a day, and Jared opened a second and then a third shop before the year was out. Seth oversaw the Petoskey operation and managed one of the new shops. Two years later Jared opened a restaurant and a clothing store and began investing in a small Ohio-based petroleum company called Standard Oil. By 1885 he was worth half a million dollars and living in an eighteen-room mansion in Highland Park, just down the street from his brother Seth.

On a September afternoon in 1914, when Jared Pink was seventy-two, a group of ornithologists was gathered around a cage at the Cincinnati zoo. Inside the cage was a passenger pigeon named Martha, and she was dying of old age. The bird gripped the wire mesh with her beak and stiffened. She was the last of her kind on earth.

> The variola virus, which causes smallpox, cannot exist
> outside the human body. It is now, as the result of pan-
> demic immunization, on the verge of extinction.

Numerous other lifeforms have disappeared in this century, among them the crested shelduck, Carolina
parakeet, Kittlitz's thrush, Molokai oo, huia, Toolach
wallaby, freckled marsupial mouse, Syrian wild ass,
Schomburgk's deer, rufous gazelle, bubal hartebeest and
Caucasian wisent.

George Robertson was infused with the spirit of Christian-
ity. When he arrived in Tasmania in 1835, the island's autochthonous population had been reduced from seven
thousand to less than two hundred in the course of the thirty-
two years that the British colony at Risdon had been in existence. The original settlers, a group of convicts under the
supervision of Lieutenant John Bowen, had hunted the native
Tasmanians as they would have hunted wolves or rats or any
other creatures that competed for space and food. George
Robertson had come to save them.

Picture him: thirty, eyes like rinse water, hair bleached
white in the sun, the tender glossy skin showing through the
molt of nose and cheekbone. A gangling tall man who walked
with a limp and carried an umbrella everywhere he went. He
was an Anglican clergyman. His superiors had sent him to the
island on a mission of mercy: to save the aboriginal Tasmanians from extinction and perdition both. Robertson had
leaped at the opportunity. He would be a paraclete, a leader,
an arm of God. But when he stepped ashore at Risdon, he
found that no one had seen a native Tasmanian—alive or
dead—in nearly five years. Like the thylacines and wombats,
they had withdrawn to the desolate slopes of the interior.

The one exception was a native woman called Trucanini
who had been captured five years earlier and integrated into
colonial life as a servant to the governor. When John Bowen
had organized a line of beaters to sweep the bush and exter-
minate the remaining "black crows," the drive had turned up

only two Tasmanians—Trucanini and her mother, who were discovered sleeping beneath a log. The others had vanished. Trucanini's mother was an old woman, blind and naked, her skin ropy and cracked. Bowen left her to die.

The day he landed, Robertson limped up to the back door of the governor's manor house, umbrella tucked under his arm, stepped into the kitchen and led Trucanini out into the courtyard. She was in her early forties, toothless, her nose splayed, cheeks and forehead whorled with tattoos. Robertson embraced her, forced her to her knees in the sand and taught her to pray. A week later the two of them struck off into the bush, unarmed, in search of the remnants of her tribe.

It took him four years. The governor had declared him legally dead, his mother back in Melbourne had been notified, a marker had been placed in the cemetery. Then one afternoon, in the teeth of a slashing monsoon, Robertson strode up the governor's teakwood steps followed by one hundred eighty-seven hungry aboriginal Christians. Wooden crosses dangled from their necks, their heads were bowed, palms layed together in prayer. The rains washed over them like a succession of waterfalls. Robertson asked for safe conduct to Flinders Island; the governor granted it.

The Tasmanians were a Stone Age society. They wore no clothes, lived in the open, foraged for food. Robertson clothed them, built huts and lean-tos, taught them to use flint, cultivate gardens, bury their excrement. He taught them to pray, and he taught them to abandon polygamy for the sacrament of marriage. They were shy, tractable people, awed and bewildered by their white redeemer, and they did their best to please him. There was one problem, however. They died like mayflies. By 1847 there were less than forty of them left. Twelve years later there were two: Trucanini, now long past menopause, and her fifth husband, William Lanne.

Robertson stuck it out, though he and Trucanini moved back into Risdon when William Lanne went off on a six-month whaling voyage. There they waited for Lanne's return, and Robertson prayed for the impossible—that Trucanini would bear a child. But then he realized that she would have to bear at least one other and then that the children would have to live in incest if the race were to survive. He no longer knew what to pray for.

When Lanne's ship dropped anchor, Robertson was waiting. He took the wizened little tattooed man by the elbow and walked him to Trucanini's hut, then waited at a discreet distance. After an hour he went home to bed. In the morning Lanne was found outside the supply store, a casket of rum and a tin cup between his legs. His head was cocked back, and his mouth, which hung open, was a caldron of flies.

Seven years later Trucanini died in bed. And George Robertson gave up the cloth.

> Concerning the higher primates: there are now on earth circa 25,000 chimpanzees, 5,000 gorillas, 3,000 orangutans, and 4,000,000,000 men.

> *Didus ineptus*, the dodo. A flightless pigeon the size of a turkey, extinct 1648. All that remains of it today is a foot in the British museum, a head in Copenhagen, and a quantity of dust.

Suns fade, and planets wither. Solar systems collapse. When the sun reaches its red-giant stage in five billion years it will flare up to sear the earth, ignite it like a torch held to a scrap of newsprint, the seas evaporated, the forests turned to ash, the ragged Himalayan peaks fused and then converted to dust, cosmic dust. What's a species here, a species there? This is where extinction becomes sublime.

Listen: when my father died I did not attend the funeral. Three years later I flew in to visit with my mother. We drank vodka gimlets, and I was suddenly seized with a desire to visit my father's grave. It was 10 P.M., December, snow fast to the frozen earth. I asked her which cemetery. She thought I was joking.

I drove as far as the heavy-link chain across the main gate, then stepped out of the car into a fine granular snow. My fingers slipped the switch of the flashlight through woolen gloves and I started for section 220F. The ground stretched off, leprous white, broken by the black scars of the monuments. It took nearly an hour to find, the granite markers alike as pebbles on a beach, names and dates, names and dates. I trailed down 220F, the light playing off stone and statue. Then I found it. My father's name in a spot of light. I regarded the name: a three-part name, identical to my own. The light held, snowflakes creeping through the beam like motes of dust. I extinguished the light.

Caye

O mother Ida, harken ere I die.—Tennyson, *Oenone*

ORLANDO'S UNCLE fathered thirty-two children. Fifteen by the first wife, five by the second, twelve by the third. Now he lives with a Canadian woman, postmenopausal. You can hear them after the generator shuts down. When the island is still and dark as a dreamless sleep, and the stone crabs crawl out of their holes.

The ground here is pocked with dark craters, burrows, veins in the earth. They are beginnings and endings. Some small as coins, others big enough to swallow a softball. The crabs creep down these orifices like the functions of the body.

Fran has a gas stove, a bed, some shelves, a battery-run tape player. She cooks. People who weren't born here can sit on the edge of the bed and eat, sip rum with her. Then

unwrinkle some bills. Fran cooks lobster, or conch, some-
times she cooks stone crab. She was not born here either, her
bed is narrow, and the batteries in the tape player are getting
weak.

Orlando sets and checks lobster traps. All the men on the
island set and check lobster traps. The traps are made of
wooden strips, shaped like Quonset huts, a conical entranceway at one end. Bait is unnecessary. The lobster, scouting the
margins of the reef, the sea chanting over him, will prowl
around this trap until he finds the conical entranceway. He
will scrabble into the trap, delighted, secure from attack. The
lobster psyche takes solace in holes. When the traps are
hauled the law requires the fishermen to release any lobster
whose tail is smaller than three inches, a seeding measure.
The fishermen do not release lobsters whose tails are smaller
than three inches—nor do they take them to market. Instead
they twist off the heads, make a welter of the sweet curled
tails, black against the frayed and blanched floorboards of
their boats, carry the bloodless white meat home to their pots.
Orlando tells me that the lobster catch is smaller this season
than it was a year ago, and that a year ago it was smaller than
the preceding season. I nod my head. Like the point of a cone
I say.

There are no roads, sidewalks, automobiles, bicycles or
shoes on the island.

Tito is a grandson of Orlando's uncle. Orlando's uncle does
not know it. The island's population is just over three
hundred. It is not surprising that a good number of the island's inhabitants should be related to Orlando's uncle, considering his energy. Tito does not live in the village, but in a
shack in the jungle on the far side of the island. He lives

alone, his eyes blue, his mother (now dead) English. Tito roams the forest with his .22, putting holes in birds and lizards. Their carcasses fertilize the soil. When he is hungry he lifts a lobster trap, spears fish, dives for conch. Or splits coconut.

The sun here is mellow as an orange. One day it will flare up and turn the solar system to cinders. Then it will fall into itself, suck in the ribbons of flame like a pale ember, gather its last breath and explode, driving particles eternally through the universe, cosmic wind.

Fran is forty, paints her toenails, wears her hair in short curls. The muscles of her abdomen are lax. She dresses in saris, halters, things of the tropics. Fifteen years ago Fran came to the island and set up residence in a ten-by-twenty-foot shack. For the first six months she had money. Afterward she cooked. Now she drinks rum beneath the bulb in her shack, finds coins for the island's children, cooks meals for visitors and occasionally for islanders. No man, tourist or islander, has been known to satisfy more than a single appetite in Fran's shack. Though not from lack of trying.

Coconut palms grow here, without (scrutable) design. The coconuts, elaborate seeds, fall to the sand like blows in the stomach. Wet from the rain, they lie cradled in the sand until one day they split. Coconut palms grow from the split coconuts, without (scrutable) design.

Tito and Ida have been observed walking hand in hand along the path to the far end of the island, the uninhabited crescent of bird and bush. In Tito's right hand, Ida's fingers; in his left, the .22. Ida's face is wide, Indian, her eyes black. Black as caverns.

Conch fritters hiss on the griddle in Fran's shack. Four lots away Orlando's uncle sits in his yard, conch shells piled high, the wedge-headed hammer and thin knife at his side, a wet conch in his lap. He presses the spiral shell to his knee and taps at it with the beak of his hammer. Twice, three times, and he's tapped a thin rectangular hole just below the point of the spiral. The knife eases in, the conch out, the shell in his hand spewing up its secrets. *Konk* he calls it.

I am sitting on the edge of Fran's bed, sipping rum, chewing lobster. There is another man in the shack, a West German. He speaks neither English nor Spanish. We eat in silence. Fran wears a halter, her belly slack, at the stove. When we finish our meal the man stands, pays, leaves. I pour another drink of rum. Fran's back is turned. I lay my hand on her flank. She tells me to leave.

In 1962 Hurricane Hilda stirred up waves thirty-five feet tall and churned them across the Caribbean in the direction of the island. The sky was smoky, dark as iron, the wind bent the trees, hurtled coconut and leaf. Tito and Ida were children, Fran was in her prime, Orlando's uncle had never heard of Canada and was yet to father four more children. The reef broke the biggest waves. All the traps were lost, the boats staved in, the shacks collapsed. Eight feet of salt water (home to lobster, conch, brine shrimp) washed over the island. Five drowned. The wind screamed blood and teeth.

The Canadian woman takes the biweekly boat to the mainland and Orlando's uncle is alone. I see him in the yard, feeding chickens and turkeys. His face is like a mud pond dried in the sun. But his hair is rich and black, he walks straight as a hoe and his arms and chest are solid. He no longer checks traps. Instead he cleans conch. Soaks the white meat in lime, sprinkles it with pepper, and exercises his aging teeth. The protein does him good.

There is no law on the island. No JP, no police, no jail.

At night I lie in my hammock, listening to the rattle of the crabs as they emerge from their burrows (dark to dark) and prowl through the scrub. I watch the sky: fronds like scissors, stars like frost. There are meteors, planets, spaces between the stars, black holes. The black holes are not visible, but there nonetheless. Stars bigger than the sun, collapsed in on themselves, with a gravitational pull that sucks in light like water down a drain. Black holes, black as the moments before birth and after death.

Ida's toes in the sand, sea wrack, the shells of conch, heads of lobster. She strolls past the boats, past the trembling docks with the outhouses perched over them, past the crude gate and the chickens and the turkeys, on up to the door of Orlando's uncle's house. Her mother is Orlando's uncle's granddaughter. She knows it, and Orlando's uncle knows it. Neither cares.

Between the shore and the reef is a stretch of about half a mile. The water is twenty or thirty feet deep, there are nests of rock, plains of sweeping thick-bladed grass, rolling like wheat in a deep wind. Among the blades, conch. The handsome flame-orange and pink shells turned to the dark bottom, the spiral peaks indicating the sky. You dive, snatch at the peaks, turn them over—they are ghostly and gray, a hole, black hole, tapped in the roof. The vacant shells frighten off the living conch, Orlando tells me, like a graveyard after dark.

Still in the afternoon heat, dogs chickens children asleep, the generator like the hum of an organ, there are cries in the air, sudden as ice, cries of passion and rhythm, the pressure of groin and groin, cries that squeeze between the planks of Orlando's uncle's shack like air escaping a brown paper bag.

Tito's shack is difficult to find in the dark. For one thing, the island is washed in night after the generator shuts down. For another, the path is narrow, not much used. If you step off the path you run the risk of snapping an ankle in the ruts dug by the stone crabs or of touching down on the carcass of a bird or lizard, sharp plumage, wet meat.

The Canadian woman was not hurt, but Orlando's uncle is dead. She'd been back two days, it was dark, she stepped out to squat and urinate. I'd heard them celebrating her return: I swung in my hammock, thinking prurient thoughts, listening. I heard the door slam, I heard the five shots. The man who came out by boat from the mainland dug a bullet from the headboard of the bed. It was a small caliber, .22 he said. He asked the islanders if any of them owned a .22. And he asked me. We knew of no one who owned a .22, we told him, and he returned to the mainland the following day. Dark and sudden, these events have adumbrated change. Fran and the Canadian woman live together now. I visit them two times a day, eat, sip rum, pay. Orlando's uncle's shack stood empty for a few weeks. Then I moved in.

Deep in the shadows I spread a towel across the ground. It is too dark to see them, but I know the holes are there, beneath the cloth, the island pocked with them like a sickness. She stretches her back there, drops her shorts. Her knees fall apart. The breeze drifts in from the sea, bare night sky above. The sand fleas are asleep. I kneel, work myself into her, poke at her mouth with my tongue. Ida, I whisper, burrowing into her, dark blood beating, rooting, thrusting, digging, deep as I can go. I want to dig deeper.

The Big Garage

For K.

B. STANDS AT THE SIDE of the highway, helpless, hands
behind his back, the droopy greatcoat like a relic of
ancient wars. There is wind and rain—or is it sleet?—and the
deadly somnolent rush of tires along the pavement. His own
vehicle rests on the shoulder, stricken somewhere in its slippery metallic heart. He does not know where, exactly, or
why—for B. is no mechanic. Far from it. In fact, he's never
built or repaired a thing in his life, never felt the restive urge
to tinker with machinery, never as a jittery adolescent dis-
mantled watches, telephone receivers, pneumatic crushers.
He is woefully unequal to the situation at hand. But wait, hold
on now—shouldn't he raise the hood, as a distress signal? Isn't
that the way it's done?

Suddenly he's in motion, glad to be doing something, con-
fronting the catastrophe, meeting the challenge. He scuttles
round to the front of the car, works his fingers under the lip of

the hood and tugs, tugs to no effect, slips in the mud, stumbles, the knees of his trousers soaked through, and then rises to tug again, shades of Buster Keaton. After sixty or seventy seconds of this it occurs to him that the catch may be inside, under the dashboard, as it was in his late wife's Volvo. There are wires—bundles of them—levers, buttons, handles, cranks and knobs in the cavern beneath the steering wheel. He had no idea. He takes a bundle of wire in his hand—each strand a different color—and thinks with a certain satisfaction of the planning and coordination that went into this machine, of the multiple factories, each dominating its own little Bavarian or American or Japanese town, of all the shifts and lunch breaks, the dies cast and what do you call them, lathes—yes, lathes—turned. All this—but more, much more. Iron ore dug from rock, hissing white hot vats of it, molten recipes, chromium, tall rubber trees, vinyl plants, crystals from the earth ground into glass. Staggering.

"Hey pal—"

B. jolted from his reverie by the harsh plosive, spasms of amber light expanding and contracting the interior of the car like the pulse of some predatory beast. Looking up into a lean face, slick hair, stoned eyes. "I was ah trying to ah get the ah latch here—"

"You'll have to ride back in the truck with me."

"Yeah, sure," B. sitting up now, confused, gripping the handle and swinging the door out to a shriek of horns and a rush of air. He cracks something in his elbow heaving it shut.

"Better get out this side."

B. slides across the seat and steps out into the mud. Behind him, the tow truck, huge, its broad bumper lowering over the hood of his neat little German-made car. He mounts the single step up into the cab and watches the impassive face of the towman as he backs round, attaches the grappling hook and hoists the rear of the car, spider and fly. A moment later the man drops into the driver's seat, door slamming with a metallic thud, gears engaging. "That'll be forty-five bucks," he says.

A white fracture of sleet caught up in the headlights, the wipers clapping, light flashing, the night a mist and a darkness beyond the windows. They've turned off the highway, jerking right and left over a succession of secondary roads, strayed so far from B.'s compass that he's long since given up any attempt at locating himself. Perhaps he's dozed even. He turns to study the crease folded into the towman's cheek. "Much farther?" he asks.

The man jerks his chin and B. looks out at a blaze of light on the dark horizon, light dropped like a stone in a pool of oil. As they draw closer he's able to distinguish a neon sign, towering letters stamped in the sky above a complex of offices, outbuildings and hangars that melts off into the shadows. Eleven or twelve sets of gas pumps, each nestled under a black steel parasol, and cars, dark and driverless, stretching across the whitening blacktop like the reverie of a used-car salesman. The sign, in neon grid, traces and retraces its colossal characters until there's no end and no beginning: GARAGE. TEGELER'S. BIG. GARAGE. TEGELER'S BIG GARAGE.

The truck pulls up in front of a deep, brightly lit office. Through the steamed-over windows B. can make out several young women, sitting legs-crossed in orange plastic chairs. From here they look like drum majorettes: white calf boots, opalescent skirts, lace frogs. And—can it be?—Dale Evans hats! What is going on here?

The towman's voice is harsh. "End of the road for you, pal."

"What about my car?"

A cigarette hangs from his lower lip like a growth, smoke squints his eyes. "Nobody here to poke into it at this hour, what do you think? I'm taking it around to Diagnosis."

"And?"

"Pfft." The man fixes him with the sort of stare you'd give a leper at the Inaugural Ball. "*And* when they get to it, they get to it."

B. steps into the fluorescent blaze of the office, coattails aflap. There are nine girls seated along the wall, left calves swollen over right knees, hands occupied with nail files, hairbrushes, barrettes, magazines. They are dressed as drum majorettes. Nappy Dale Evans hats perch atop their layered cuts, short-and-sassies, blown curls. All nine look up and smile. Then a short redhead rises, and sweet as a mother superior welcoming a novice, asks if she can be of service.

B. is confused. "It . . . it's my car," he says.

"Ohhh," running her tongue round her lips. "You're the Audi."

"Right."

"Just wait a sec and I'll ring Diagnosis," she says, highstepping across the room to an intercom panel set in the wall. At that moment a buzzer sounds in the office and a car pulls up to the farthest set of gas pumps. The redhead jerks to a halt, peers out the window, curses, shrugs into a fringed suede jacket and hurries out into the storm. B. locks fingers behind his back and waits. He rocks on his feet, whistles sotto voce, casts furtive glances at the knee-down of the eight majorettes. The droopy greatcoat, soaked through, feels like an American black bear (*Ursus americanus*) hanging round his neck.

Then the door heaves back on its hinges and the redhead reappears, stamping round the doormat, shaking out the jacket, knocking the Stetson against her thigh. "Brrrr," she says. In her hand, a clutch of bills. She marches over to the cash register and deposits them, then takes her seat at the far end of the line of majorettes. B. continues to rock on his feet.

He clears his throat. Finally he ambles across the room and stops in front of her chair. "Ahh . . ."

She looks up. "Yes? Can I help you?"

"You were going to call Diagnosis about my car?"

"Oh," grimacing. "No need to bother. Why at this hour they're long closed up. You'll have to wait till morning."

"But a minute ago—"

"No, no sense at all. The Head Diagnostician leaves at five, and here it's nearly ten. And his staff gets off at five-thirty. The best we could hope for is a shop steward—and what would he know? Ha. If I rang up now I'd be lucky to get hold of a janitor." She settles back in her chair and leafs through a magazine. Then she looks up again. "Listen. If you want some advice, there's a pay phone in the anteroom. Better call somebody to come get you."

The girl has a point there. It's late already and arrangements will have to be made about getting to work in the morning. The dog needs walking, the cat feeding. And all these hassles have sapped him to the point where all he wants from life is sleep and forgetfulness. But there's no one to call, really. Except possibly Dora—Dora Ouzel, the gay divorcée he's been dating since his wife's accident.

One of the majorettes yawns. Another blows a puff of detritus from her nail file. "Ho hum," says the redhead.

B. steps into the anteroom, searches through his pockets for change, and forgets Dora's number. He paws through the phone book, but the names of the towns seem unfamiliar and he can't seem to find Dora's listing. He makes an effort of memory and dials.

"Hello?"

"Hello, Dora? —B. Listen, I hate to disturb you at this hour but—"

"Are you all right?"

"Yes, I'm fine."

"That's nice, I'm fine too. But no matter how you slice it my name ain't Dora."

"You're not Dora?"

"No, but you're B., aren't you?"

"Yes . . . but how did you know?"

"You told me. You said: 'Hello, Dora? —B.' . . . and then you tried to come on with some phony excuse for forgetting our date tonight or is it that you're out hooching it up and you want me—if I was Dora and I bless my stars I'm not—to come out in this hellish weather that isn't fit for a damn dog for christsake and risk my bones and bladder to drive you home because only one person inhabits your solipsistic universe— *You* with a capital Y—and *You* have drunk yourself into a blithering stupor. You know what I got to say to you, buster? Take a flyer. Ha, ha, ha."

There is a click at the other end of the line. In the movies heroes say "Hello, hello, hello," in situations like this, but B., dispirited, the greatcoat beginning to reek a bit in the confines of the antechamber, only reaches out to replace the receiver in its cradle.

Back in the office B. is confronted with eight empty chairs. The redhead occupies the ninth, legs crossed, hat in lap, curls flaring round the cover of her magazine like a solar phenomenon. Where five minutes earlier there were enough majorettes to front a battle of the bands, there is now only one. She glances up as the door slams behind him. "Any luck?"

B. is suddenly overwhelmed with exhaustion. He's just gone fifteen rounds, scaled Everest, staggered out of the Channel at Calais. "No," he whispers.

"Well that really is too bad. All the other girls go home at ten and I'm sure any one of them would have been happy to give you a lift. . . . You know it really is a pity the way some of you men handle your affairs. Why if I had as little common sense as you I wouldn't last ten minutes on this job."

B. heaves himself down on one of the plastic chairs. Somehow, somewhere along the line, his sense of proportion has begun to erode. He blows his nose lugubriously. Then hides behind his hands and massages his eyes.

"Come on now." The girl's voice is soft, conciliatory. She is standing over him, her hand stretched out to his. "I'll fix you up a place to sleep in the back of the shop."

The redhead (her name is Rita—B. thought to ask as a sort of quid pro quo for her offer of a place to sleep) leads him through a narrow passageway which gives on to an immense darkened hangar. B. hunches in the greatcoat, flips up his collar and follows her into the echo-haunted reaches. Their footsteps clap up to the rafters, blind birds beating at the roof, echoing and reechoing in the darkness. There is a chill as of open spaces, a stink of raw metal, oil, sludge. Rita is up ahead, her white boots ghostly in the dark. "Watch your step," she cautions, but B. has already encountered some impenetrable, rock-hard hazard, barked his shin and pitched forward into what seems to be an open grease pit.

"Hurt yourself?"

B. lies there silent—frustrated, childish, perverse.

"B.? Answer me—are you all right?"

He will lie here, dumb as a block, till the Andes are nubs and the moon melts from the sky. But then suddenly the cavern blooms with light (a brown crepuscular light, it's true, but light just the same) and the game's up.

"So there you are!" Arms akimbo, a grin on her face. "Now get yourself up out of there and stop your sulking. I can't play games all night you know. There's eleven sets of pumps out there I'm responsible for."

B. finds himself sprawled all over an engine block, grease-slicked and massive, that must have come out of a Sherman tank. But it's the hangar, lit like the grainy daguerreotype of a Civil War battlefield, that really interests him. The sheer expanse of the place! And the cars, thousands of them, stretching all the way down to the dark V at the far end of the building. Bugattis, Morrises, La Salles, Daimlers, the back end of a Pierce-Arrow, a Stutz Bearcat. The rounded humps of tops and fenders, tarnished bumpers, hoods thrown open like gaping mouths. Engines swing on cables, blackened grills and punctured cloth tops gather in the corners, a Duesenberg, its interior gutted, squats over a trench in the concrete.

"Pretty amazing, huh?" Rita says, reaching out a hand to help him up. "This is Geriatrics. Mainly foreign. You should see the Contemp wings."

"But what do you do with all these—?"

"Oh, we fix them. At least the technicians and mechanics do."

There is something wrong here, something amiss. B. can feel it nagging at the edges of his consciousness . . . but then he really is dog-tired. Rita has him by the hand. They amble past a couple hundred cars, dust-embossed, ribs and bones showing, windshields black as ground-out eyes. Now he has it: "But if you fix them, what are they doing here?"

Rita stops dead to look him in the eye, frowning, schoolmarmish. "These things take time, you know." She sighs. "What do you think: they do it overnight?"

The back room is the size of a storage closet. In fact, it is a storage closet, fitted out with cots. When Rita flicks the light switch B. is shocked to discover three other people occupying the makeshift dormitory: two men in rumpled suits and a middle-aged woman in a rumpled print dress. One of the men sits up and rubs his eyes. His tie is loose, shirt filthy, a patchy beard maculating his cheeks. He mumbles something—B. catches the words "drive shaft"—and then turns his face back to the cot, already sucking in breath for the first stertorous blast: hkk-hkk-hkkkkkkgg.

"What the hell is this?" B. is astonished, scandalized, cranky and tired. Tools and blackened rags lie scattered over the concrete floor, dulled jars of bolts and screws and wing nuts line the shelves. A number of unfolded cots, their fabric stained and grease-spotted, stand in the corner.

"This is where you sleep, silly."

"But—who?"

"It's obvious, isn't it? They're customers, like yourself, waiting for their cars. The man in brown is the Gremlin, the one with the beard is the Cougar—no, I'm sorry, the woman is the Cougar—he's the Citroën."

B. is appalled. "And I'm the Audi, is that it?"

Suddenly Rita is in his arms, the smooth satiny feel of her uniform, the sticky warmth of her breath. "You're more to me than a machine, B. Do you know that I like you? Alot." And then he finds himself nuzzling her ear, the downy ridge of her jawbone. She presses against him, he fumbles under the cheerleader's tutu for the slippery underthings. One of the sleepers groans, but B. is lost, oblivious, tugging and massaging like a horny teenager. Rita reaches behind to unzip her uniform, the long smooth arch of her back, shoulders and arms shedding the opalescent rayon like a holiday on ice when suddenly a buzzer sounds—loud and brash—end of the round, change classes, dive for shelter.

Rita freezes, then bursts into motion. "A customer!" she pants, and then she's gone. B. watches her callipygian form recede into the gloom of the Geriatrics Section, the sharp projection in his trousers receding with her, until she touches

the light switch and vanishes in darkness. B. trundles back
into the closet, selects a cot, and falls into an exploratory
darkness of his own.

B.'s breath is a puff of cotton as he wakes to the chill gloom
of the storage closet and the sound of tools grating, whining
and racheting somewhere off in the distance. At first he can't
locate himself—What the? Where?—but the odors of gas and
kerosene and motor oil bring him back. He is stranded at
Tegeler's Big Garage, it is a workday, he has been sleeping
with strangers, his car is nonfunctional. B. lurches up from
the cot with a gasp—only to find that he's being watched. It is
the man with the patchy beard and rancid shirt. He is sitting
on the edge of a cot, stirring coffee in a cardboard container,
his eyes fixed on B. My checkbook, my wallet, my wristwatch,
thinks B.

"Mornin'," the man says. "My name's Rusty," holding out
his hand. The others—the man in brown (or was it gray?) and
the Cougar woman—are gone.

B. shakes the man's hand. "Name's B.," he says, somewhere between wary and paranoid. "How do I get out of
here?"

"Your first day, huh?"

"What do you mean?" B. detects an edge of hysteria slicing
through his voice, as if it belonged to someone else in some
other situation. A pistol-whipped actress in a TV melodrama,
for instance.

"No need to get excited," Rusty says. "I know how dis-
quieting that first day can be. Why Cougar here—that woman
in the print dress slept with us last night?—she sniveled and
whimpered the whole time her first night here. Shit. It was
like being in a bomb shelter or some frigging thing. Sure, I
know how it is. You got a routine—job, wife at home, kids
maybe, dog, cat, goldfish—and naturally you're anxious to get

back to it. Well let me give you some advice. I been here six days already and I still haven't even got an appointment lined up with the Appointments Secretary so's I can get in to see the Assistant to the Head Diagnostician, Imports Division, and find out what's wrong with my car. So look: don't work up no ulcer over the thing. Just make your application and sit tight."

The man is an escapee, that's it, an escapee from an institution for the terminally, unconditionally and abysmally insane. B. hangs tough. "You expect me to believe that cock-and-bull story? If you're so desperate why don't you call a cab?"

"Taxis don't run this far out."

"Bus?"

"No buses in this district."

"Surely you've got friends to call—"

"Tried it, couldn't get through. Busy signals, recordings, wrong numbers. Finally got through to Theotis Stover two nights ago. Said he'd come out but his car's broke down."

"You could hitchhike."

"Spent six hours out there my first day. Twelve degrees F. Nobody even slowed down. Besides, even if I could get home, what then? Can't get to work, can't buy food. No sir. I'm staying right here till I get that car back."

B. cannot accept it. The whole thing is absurd. He's on him like F. Lee Bailey grilling a shaky witness. "What about the girls in the main office? They'll take you—one of them told me so."

"They take you?"

"No, but—"

"Look: they say that to be accommodating, don't you see? I mean we *are* customers after all. But they can't give you a lift—it's their job if they do."

"You mean—?"

"That's right. And wait'll you see the bill when you finally do get out of here. Word is that cot you're sitting on goes for twelve bucks a night."

The bastards. It could be weeks here. He'll lose his job, the animals'll tear up the rugs, piss in the bed and finally, starved, the dog will turn on the cat. . . . B. looks up, a new worry on his lips: "But what do you eat here?"

Rusty rises. "C'mon, I'll show you the ropes." B. follows him out into the half-lit and silent hangar, past the ranks of ruined automobiles, the mounds of tires and tools. "Breakfast is out of the machines. They got coffee, hot chocolate, candy bars, cross-ants and cigarettes. Lunch and late afternoon snack you get down at the Mechanics' Cafeteria." Rusty's voice booms and echoes through the wide open spaces till B. begins to feel surrounded. Overhead, the morning cowers against the grimed skylights. "And eat your fill," Rusty adds, "—it all goes on the tab."

The office is bright as a cathedral with a miracle in progress. B. squints into the sunlight and recognizes the swaying ankles of a squad of majorettes. He asks for Rita, finds she's off till six at night. Outside, the sound of scraping, the putt-putt of snowplow jeeps. B. glances up. Oh, shit. There must be a foot and a half of snow on the ground.

The girls are chewing gum and sipping coffee from personalized mugs: Mary-Alice, Valerie, Beatrice, Lulu. B. hunches in the greatcoat, confused, until Rusty bums a dollar and hands him a cup of coffee. Slurping and blowing, B. stands at the window and watches an old man stoop over an aluminum snow shovel. Jets of fog stream from the old man's nostrils, ice cakes his mustache.

"Criminal, ain't it?" says Rusty.

"What?"

"The old man out there. That's Tegeler's father, seventy-some-odd years old. Tegeler makes him earn his keep, sweeping up, clearing snow, polishing the pumps."

"No!" B. is stupefied.

"Yeah, he's some hardnose, Tegeler. And I'll tell you something else too—he's set up better than Onassis and Rockefeller put together. See that lot across the street?"

B. looks. TEGELER'S BIG LOT. How'd he miss that?

"They sell new Tegelers there."

"Tegelers?"

"Yeah—he's got his own company: the Tegeler Motor Works. Real lemons from what I hear. . . . But will you look what time it is!" Rusty slaps his forehead. "We got to get down to Appointments or we'll both grow old in this place."

The Appointments Office, like the reward chamber in a rat maze, is located at the far end of a complicated network of passageways, crossways and counterways. It is a large carpeted room with desks, potted plants and tellers' windows, not at all unlike a branch bank. The Cougar woman and the man in the brown suit are there, waiting, along with a number of others, all of them looking bedraggled and harassed. Rusty enters deferentially and takes a seat beside Brown Suit, but B. strides across the room to where a hopelessly walleyed woman sits at a desk, riffling through a bundle of papers. "Excuse me," he says.

The woman looks up, her left iris drowning in white.

"I'm here—" B. breaks off, confused as to which eye to address: alternately one and then the other seems to be scrutinizing him. Finally he zeroes in on her nose and continues: "—about my car. I—"

"Do you have an appointment?"

"No, I don't. But you see I'm a busy man, and I depend entirely on the car for transportation and—"

"Don't we all?"

"—and I've already missed a day of work." B. gives her a doleful look, a look charged with chagrin for so thwarting the work ethic and weakening the national fiber. "I've got to have it seen to as soon as possible. If not sooner." Ending with a broad grin, the bon mot just the thing to break the ice.

"Yes," she says, heaving a great wet sigh. "I understand your anxiety and I sympathize with you, I really do. But," the left pupil working round to glare at him now, "I can't say I think much of the way you conduct yourself—barging in here and exalting your own selfish concerns above those of the others here. Do you think that there's no one else in the world but you? No other ailing auto but yours? Does Tegeler's Big Garage operate for fifty-nine years, employing hundreds of people, constantly expanding, improving, streamlining its operations, only to prepare itself for the eventuality of your breakdown? Tsssss! I'm afraid, my friend, that your arrogant egotism knows no bounds."

B. hangs his head, shuffles his feet, the greatcoat impossibly warm.

"Now. You'll have to fill out the application for an appointment and wait your turn with the others. Though you really haven't shown anything to deserve it, I think you may have a bit of luck today after all. The Secretary left word that he'd be in at three this afternoon."

B. takes a seat beside the Cougar woman and stares down at the form in his hand as if it were a loaded .44. He is dazed, still tingling from the vehemence of the secretary's attack. The form is seven pages long. There are questions about employment, annual income, collateral, next of kin. Page 4 is devoted to physical inquiries: ever had measles? leprosy? irregularity? The next delves deeper: do you feel that people are out to get you? why do you hate your father? The form ends up with two pages of IQ stuff: if a farmer has 200 acres and devotes 1/16 of his land to soybeans, 5/8 to corn and 1/3 to sugar beets, how much does he have left for a drive-in movie? B. glances over at the Cougar woman. Her lower lip is thrust forward, a blackened stub of pencil twists in her fingers, an appointment form, scrawled over in pencil with circled red corrections, lies in her lap. Suddenly B. is on his feet and stalking out the door, fragments of paper sifting down in his wake like confetti. Behind him, the sound of collective gasping.

Out in the corridor B. collars a man in spattered blue coveralls and asks him where the Imports Division is. The man, squat, swarthy, mustachioed, looks at him blank as a cow. "No entiendo," he says.

"The. Imports. Division."

"No hablo inglés—y no me gustan las preguntas de cabrónes tontos." The man shrugs his shoulder out from under B.'s palm and struts off down the hall like a ruffled rooster. But B. is encouraged: Imports must be close at hand. He hurries off in the direction from which the man came (was he Italian or only a Puerto Rican?), following the corridor around to the left, past connecting hallways clogged with mechanics and white-smocked technicians, following it right on up to a steel fire door with the words NO ADMITTANCE stamped across it in admonitory red. There is a moment of hesitation . . . then he twists the knob and steps in.

"Was ist das?" A workman looks up at him, screwdriver in hand, expression modulating from surprise to menace. B. finds himself in another hangar, gloomy and expansive as the first, electric tools screeching like an army of mechanical crickets. But what's this?: he's surrounded by late-model cars—German cars—Beetles, Foxes, Rabbits, sleek Mercedes sedans! Not only has he stumbled across the Imports Division, but luck or instinct or good looks has guided him right to German Specialities. Well, ha-cha! He's squinting down the rows of cars, hoping to catch sight of his own, when he feels a pressure on his arm. It is the workman with the screwdriver. "Vot you vant?" he demands.

"Uh—have you got an Audi in here? Powder blue with a black vinyl top?"

The workman is in his early twenties. He is tall and obscenely corpulent. Skin pale as the moon, jowls reddening as if with a rash, white hair cropped across his ears and pinched beneath a preposterously undersized engineer's cap. He tightens his grip on B.'s arm and calls out into the gloom—"Holger! Friedrich!"—his voice reverberating through the vault like the battle cry of some Mesozoic monster.

Two men, flaxen-haired, in work clothes and caps, step from the shadows. Each grips a crescent wrench big as the jawbone of an ass. "Was gibt es, Klaus?"

"Mein Herr vants to know haff we got und *Aw*-dee."

"How do you say it?" The two newcomers are standing over him now, the one in the wire-rimmed spectacles leering into his eyes.

"Audi," B. says. "A German-made car?"

"Aw-dee? No, never heard of such a car," the man says. "A cowboy maybe—family name of Murphy?"

Klaus laughs, "Har-har-har," booming at the ceiling. The other fellow, short, scar on his cheek, joins in with a psychopathic snicker. Wire-rims grins.

Oh, oh.

"Listen," B. says, a whining edge to his voice, "I know I'm not supposed to be in here but I saw no other way of—"

"Cutting trew der bullshit," says Wire-rims.

"Yes, and finding out what's wrong—"

"On a grassroot level," interjects the snickerer.

"—right, at the grassroot level, by coming directly to you. I'm getting desperate. Really. That car is my life's breath itself. And I don't mean to get dramatic or anything, but I just can't survive without it."

"Ja," says Wire-rims, "you haff come to der right men. We haff your car, wery serious. Ja. Der bratwurst assembly broke down and we haff sent out immediately for a brötchen und mustard." This time all three break into laughter, Klaus booming, the snickerer snickering, Wire-rims pinching his lips and emitting a high-pitched hoo-hoo-hoo.

"No, *seriously*," says B.

"You vant to get serious? Okay, we get serious. On your car we do a compression check, we put new solenoids in der U joints und we push der push rods," says Wire-rims.

"Ja. Und we see you need a new vertical stabilizer, head gasket und PCV valve," rasps the snickerer.

"Your sump leaks."

"Bearings knock."

"Plugs misfire."

B. has had enough. "Wiseguys!" he shouts. "I'll report you to your superiors!" But far from daunting them, his outburst has the opposite effect. Viz., Klaus grabs him by the collar and breathes beer and sauerbraten in his face. "We are Chermans," he hisses, "—we haff no superiors."

"Und dammit punktum!" bellows the snickerer. "Enough of dis twaddle. We haff no car of yours und furdermore we suspect you of telling to us fibs in order maybe to misappropriate the vehicle of some otter person."

"For shame," says Wire-rims.

"Vat shall we do mit him?" the snickerer hisses.

"I am tinking he maybe needs a little lubrication," says

Wire-rims. "No sense of humor, wery dry." He produces a
grease gun from behind his back.

And then, for the first time in his life, B. is decorated—
down his collar, up his sleeve, crosshatched over his
lapels—in ropy, cake-frosting strings of grease, while Klaus
howls like a terminally tickled child and the snickerer's eyes
flash. A moment later he finds himself lofted into the air,
strange hands at his armpits and thighs, swinging to and fro
before the gaping black mouth of a laundry chute—"Zum
ersten! zum andern! zum dritten!"—and then he's airborne,
and things get very dark indeed.

B. is lying facedown in an avalanche of cloth: grimy rags,
stiffened chamois, socks and undershorts yellowed with age
and sweat and worse, handkerchiefs congealed with sputum,
coveralls wet with oil. He is stung with humiliation and outrage. He's been cozened, humbugged, duped, gulled,
spurned, insulted, ignored and now finally assaulted. There'll
be lawsuits, damn them, letters to Congressmen—but for
now, if he's to salvage a scrap of self-respect, he's got to get
out of here. He sits up, peels a sock from his face, and discov-
ers the interior of a tiny room, a room no bigger than a laundry closet. It is warm, hot even.

Two doors open onto the closet. The one to the left is
wreathed in steam, pale shoots and tendrils of it curling
through the keyhole, under the jamb. B. throws back the door
and is enveloped in fog. He is confused. The Minotaur's
labyrinth? Ship at sea? House afire? He can see nothing, the
sound of machinery straining at his ears, moisture beading
along eyebrows, nostril hairs, cowlick. Then it occurs to him:
the carwash! Of course. And the carwash must give onto the
parking lot, which in turn gives onto the highway. He'll simply duck through it and then hitchhike—or if worse comes to

worst—walk—until he either makes it home or perishes in the attempt.

B. steps through the door and is instantly flattened by a mammoth, water-spewing pom-pom. He tries to get to his feet, but the sleeve of his coat seems to be caught in some sort of runner or track—and now the whole apparatus is jerking forward, gears whirring and clicking somewhere off in the mist. B., struggling to free the coat, finds himself jerking along with it. The mechanism heaves forward, dragging B. through an extended puddle of mud, suds and road salt. A jet of water flushes the right side of his face, a second pom-pom lumbers out of the haze and pins his chest to the floor, something tears the shoe from his right foot. Soap in his ears, down his neck, sudsing and sudsing: and now a giant cylinder, a mill wheel covered with sponges, descends and rakes the length of his body. B. shouts for help, but the machinery grinds on, squeaking and racheting, war of the worlds. Look out!: cold rinse. He holds his breath, glacial runoff coursing over his body, a bitter pill. Then there's a liberal basting with hot wax, the clouds part, and the machine turns him loose with a jolt in the rear that tumbles him out the bay door and onto the slick permafrost of the parking lot.

He staggers to his feet. There's a savage pain in his lower back and his right shoulder has got to be dislocated. No matter: he forges on. Round the outbuildings, past the front office and on out to the highway.

It has begun to get dark. B., hair frozen to his scalp, shoeless, the greatcoat stiff as a dried fish, limps along the highway no more than a mile from the garage. All around him, far as he can see, is wasteland: crop-stubble swallowed in drifts, the stripped branches of the deciduous trees, rusty barbed wire. Not even a farmhouse on the horizon. Nothing. He'd feel like

Peary running for the Pole but for the twin beacons of Garage
and Lot at his back.

Suddenly a fitful light wavers out over the road—a car
coming toward him! (He's been out here for hours, holding
out his thumb, hobbling along. The first ride took him south
of Tegeler's about two miles—a farmer, turning off into
nowhere. The second—he didn't care which direction he
went in, just wanted to get out of the cold—took him back
north about three miles. Another farmer. Kissin' cousin to the
first, no doubt. Ha, ha.)

B. crosses the road and holds out his thumb. He is dancing
with cold, clonic, shoulder, arm, wrist and extended thumb
jerking like the checkered flag at the finish of the Grand Prix.
Stop, he whispers, teeth clicking like dice, stop, please God
stop. Light floods his face for an instant, and then it's gone.
But wait—they're stopping! Snot crusted to his lip, shoe in
hand, B. double-times up to the waiting car, throws back the
door and leaps in.

"B.! What's happened?"

It is Rita. Thank God.

"R-r-r-r-ita?" he stammers, body racked with tremors, the
seatsprings chattering under him. "The ma-ma-machine."

"Machine? What are you talking about?"

"I-I need a rrr-ride. Wh-where you going?" B. manages,
falling into a sneezing jag.

Rita puts the car in gear, the tires grab hold of the pavement. "Why—to work, of course."

The others smack their lips, sigh, snore, toss on their cots.
Rusty, Brown Suit, the Cougar woman. B. lies there listening
to them, staring into the darkness. His own breathing comes
hard (TB, pleurisy, pneumonia—bronchitis at the very least).
Rita—good old Rita—has filled him full of hot coffee and
schnapps, given him a brace of cold pills and put him to bed.

He is thoroughly miserable of course—the car riding his mind like a bogey, health shot, job lost, pets starved—but the snugness of the blanket and dry mechanic's uniform Rita has found for him, combined with the country-sunset glow of the schnapps, is seducing him off to sleep. It is very still. The smell of turpentine hangs in the air. He pulls the blanket up to his nose.

Suddenly the light flicks on. It is Rita, all thighs and calves in her majorette's outfit. But what's this? There's a man with her, a stranger. "Is this it?" the man says.

"Well of course it is, silly."

"But who are these chibonies?"

"It's obvious isn't it? They're customers, like yourself, waiting for their cars. The man in brown is the Gremlin, the one with the beard is the Citroën, the woman is the Cougar and the old guy on the end is the Audi."

"And I'm the Jaguar, is that it?"

"You're more to me than a machine, Jeff. Do you know that I like you? Alot."

B. is mortally wounded. Enemy flak, they've hit him in the guts. He squeezes his eyes shut, stops his ears, but he can hear them just the same: heavy breathing, a moan soft as fur, the rush of zippers. But then the buzzer sounds and Rita gasps. "A customer!" she squeals, struggling back into her clothes and then hurrying off through the Geriatrics hangar, her footsteps like pinpricks along the spine. "Hey!" the new guy bellows. But she's gone.

The new guy sighs, then selects a cot and beds down beside B. B. can hear him removing his things, gargling from a bottle, whispering prayers to himself—"Bless Mama, Uncle Ernie, Bear Bryant . . ."—then the room dashes into darkness and B. can open his eyes.

He fights back a cough. His heart is hammering. He thinks how pleasant it would be to die . . . but then thinks how pleasant it would be to step through the door of his apartment again, take a hot shower and crawl into bed. It is then that the vision comes to him—a waking dream—shot through with color and movement and depth. He sees Tegeler's Big Lot, the ranks of cars, new Tegelers, lines of variegated color like beads on a string, windshields glinting in the sun, antennae jabbing at the sky, stiff and erect, like the swords of a conquering army . . .

In the dark, beneath the blanket, he reaches for his checkbook.

Green Hell

THERE HAS BEEN a collision (with birds, black flocks of them), an announcement from the pilot's cabin, a moment of abeyed hysteria, and then the downward rush. The plane is nosing for the ground at a forty-five-degree angle, engines wheezing, spewing smoke and feathers. Lights flash, breathing apparatus drops and dangles. Our drinks become lariats, the glasses knives. Lunch (chicken croquettes, gravy, reconstituted potatoes and imitation cranberry sauce) decorates our shirts and vests. Outside there is the shriek of the air over the wings; inside, the rock-dust rumble of grinding teeth, molar on molar. My face seems to be slipping over my head like a rubber mask. And then, horribly, the first trees become visible beyond the windows. We gasp once and then we're down, skidding through the greenery, jolted from our seats, panicked, repentant, savage. Windows strain and pop like light bulbs. We lose our bowels. The plane grates through the trees, the shriek of branches like the keen of harpies along the fuselage, our bodies jarred, dashed and knocked like the silver balls in a pinball machine. And then suddenly it's over: we are stopped (think of a high diver meeting the board on the way down). I expect (have expected) flames.

There are no flames. There is blood. Thick clots of it, puddles, ponds, lakes. We count heads. Eight of us still have them: myself, the professor, the pilot (his arm already bound up in a sparkling white sling), the mime, Tanqueray with a twist (nothing worse than a gin drinker), the man allergic to cats (runny eyes, red nose), the cat breeder, and Andrea, the stewardess. The cats, to a one, have survived. They crouch in their cages, coated with wet kitty litter like tempura shrimp. The rugby players, all twelve of them (dark-faced, scowling sorts), are dead. Perhaps just as well.

Dazed, palms pressed to bruised organs, handkerchiefs dabbing at wounds, we hobble from the wreckage. Tanqueray is sniveling, a soft moan and gargle like rain on the roof and down the gutter. The mime makes an Emmett Kelly face. The professor limps, cradling a black briefcase with *Fiskeridirektoratets Havforskningsinstitutt* engraved in the corner. The cats, left aboard, begin to yowl. The allergic man throws back his head, sneezes.

We look around: trees that go up three hundred feet, lianas, leaves the size of shower curtains, weeds thick as a knit sweater. Step back ten feet and the plane disappears. The pilot breaks the news: we've come down in the heart of the Amazon basin, hundreds perhaps thousands of miles from the nearest toilet.

The radio, of course, is dead.

Evening

We are back in the plane. They've sopped up the gore, switched the seats with palm fronds, buried the rugby players. Air freshener has been sprayed. The punctures (sardine tin, church key) have been plugged with life preservers, rubber life rafts. This then, will be our shelter.

Andrea, her uniform torn over the breast and slit up the leg, portions out our dinner: two of those plastic thimbles of nondairy creamer, a petrified brioche, two plastic packets of Thousand Island dressing, a cup of water and Bloody Mary mix. Apiece.

"Life has its little rewards," says Tanqueray, smacking his lips. He is a man of sagging flesh, torrid complexion, drooping into his sixth decade. There are two empty gin bottles (miniatures) on his tray.

The professor looks up at him. He pages rapidly through a Norwegian–English dictionary. "Good evening," he says. "I am well. And you?"

Tanqueray nods.

"I sink we come rain," the professor says.

The allergic man rattles a bottle of pills.

The mime makes a show of licking the plastic recesses of his Thousand Island packet.

"Foreigner, eh?" says Tanqueray.

Suddenly the pilot is on his feet. "Now listen, everybody," he booms. "I'm going to lay it on the line. No mincing words, no pussyfooting. We're in a jam. No food, no water, no medical supplies. I'm not saying we're not lucky to be alive and I'm not saying that me and the prof here ain't going to try our damndest to get this crate in the air again . . . but I am saying we're in a jam. If we stick together, if we fight this thing—if we work like a team—we'll make it."

I watch him: the curls at his temple, sharp nose, white teeth, the set of his jaw (prognathic). I realize that we have a leader. I further realize that I detest him. I doubt that we will make it.

"A team," he repeats.

The mime makes his George-Washington-crossing-the-Delaware face.

Night

Chiggers, ticks, gnats, nits. Cicadas. Millipedes, centipedes, omnipedes, minipedes, pincerheads, poison toads, land leeches, skinks. Palmetto bugs. Iguanas, fer-de-lance, wolf spiders, diggers, buzzers, hissers, stinkers. Oonipids. Spitting spiders. Ants. Mites. Flits. Whips. Mosquitoes.

Morning

The gloom brightens beyond the shattered plastic windows. Things are cooing and chattering in the bushes. Weep-weep-weep. Coo-hooo, coo-hooo. I wake itching. There is a spider the size of a two-egg omelet on my chest. When I lift my hand (slowly and stealthily, like a tropism) he scrambles across my face and up over the seat.

Tanqueray (buttery-faced, pouchy slob) is snoring. I sit up. The cat man is watching me. "Good morning," he whispers. The lower half of his face, from the lips down, is the color of a plum. A birthmark. I'd taken it for a beard, but now, up close, I see the mistake.

"Sleep well?" he whispers.

I grunt, scratch.

The others are still sleeping. I can hear the professor grinding his teeth, the allergic man wheezing. Andrea and the pilot are not present. The door to the pilot's cabin is drawn shut. Somewhere, a cat wails.

"Hssst," says the cat man. He stands, beckons with a finger, then slips out the door. I follow.

Things hiss off in the vegetation and rattle in the trees. We slash our way to the baggage compartment, where the cat man pauses to lift the door and duck his way in. Immediately I become aware of the distinctive odor attaching to the feline body functions. I step inside.

"My beauties," says the cat man, addressing the cats. They yowl in unison and he croons to them ("little ones," "prettyfeet," "buttertails") in a primitive sort of recognition rite. I realize that the cat man is an ass.

"Let me introduce you to my wards," he says. "This"— there is a cat in his arms, its fur like cotton candy—"is Egmont. He's a Chinchilla Persian. Best of Show at Rio two weeks ago. I wouldn't take ten thousand dollars for him." He looks at me. I whistle, gauging the appropriate response. He points to the cages successively: "Joy Boy, Roos, Great Northern, Peaker and Peaker II. Roos is an Aroostook Maine Moon Cat."

"Very nice," I say, trying to picture the man as a ten-year-old hounded into a wimpy affection for cats by the tough kids, merciless on the subject of his purple face. But then suddenly my nostrils charge. He is twisting the key on a tin of herring.

"Special diet," he says. "For their coats."

Real food has not passed my lips in over twenty-four hours. At his feet, a cardboard box packed with cans: baby smoked oysters, sardines, anchovies, salmon, tuna. When he turns to feed Joy Boy I fill my pockets.

He sighs. "Gorgeous, aren't they?"

"Yes," I say. With feeling.

Afternoon

We have had a meeting. Certain propositions have been carried. Namely, that we are a society in microcosm. That tasks will be (equably) apportioned. That we will work toward a common goal. As a team.

The pilot addressed us (slingless). He spoke with the microphone at his lips, out of habit I suppose, and with his Pan Am captain's cap raked across one eyebrow. Andrea stood at his side, her fingers twined in his, her uniform like a fishnet. The rest of us occupied our seats (locked in the upright position), our seat belts fastened, not smoking. We itched, sweated, squirmed. The pilot talked of the spirit of democracy, the social contract, the state of nature, the myth of the noble savage and the mythopoeic significance of Uncle Sam. He also dwelt on the term *pilot* as image, and explored its etymology. Then, in a voice vote (yea/nay), we elected him leader.

He proceeded to assign duties. He, the pilot, would oversee food and water supplies. At the same time, he and the professor would tinker with the engine and tighten bolts. Andrea would hold their tools. The mime's job was to write our constitution. Tanqueray would see that the miniatures were emptied. (He interjected here to indicate that he would cheerfully take on the task appointed him, though it would entail tackling the inferior spirits as well as gin—taking the bad with the good, as he put it. The pilot found him out of order but made note of the comment in any case.) To the allergic man (who sagged, red and wheezing) fell the duty of keeping things tidy within the plane. The cat man and myself were designated food gatherers, with the attendant task of clearing a landing strip. Then the pilot threw the meeting open to comments from the floor.

The allergic man stood, wiping his eyes. "I insist," he said, and then fell into a coughing spasm, unable to continue until the mime delivered a number of slaps to his back with the even, flat strokes of a man beating a carpet. "I insist that the obscene, dander-spewing vermin in the baggage compartment be removed from the immediate vicinity of the aircraft." (These were the first articulate sounds he had produced. Judging from diction, cadence and the accent in which they were delivered, it began to occur to me that he must be an Englishman. My father was an Englishman. I have an unreasoning, inexorable and violent loathing for all things English.) "In fact," he continued, choking into his handkerchief, "I should like to see all the squirrelly little beggars spitted and roasted like hares, what with the state of our food supply."

The cat man's purple shaded to black. He unbuckled his seat belt, stood, stepped over to the English/allergic man, and put a fist in his eye. The pilot called the cat man out of order, and with the aid of Tanqueray and the professor, ejected him from the meeting. Oaths were exchanged. Outside, in the bush, a howler monkey imitated the shriek of a jaguar set afire.

The pilot adjourned the meeting.

Evening

It is almost pleasant: sun firing the highest leaves, flowers and vines and bearded Spanish moss like a Rousseau exhibit, the spit and crackle of the campfire, the sweet strong odor of roasting meat. Joy Boy and Peaker II are turning on spits. The cat man has been exiled, the spoils (fat pampered feline) confiscated. Much to my chagrin, he thought to make off with his cache of cat food, and had actually set loose Egmont, Peaker, Roos and Great Northern before the pilot could get to him. I told no one of the cat food. Eleven shiny tins of it lie buried not twenty feet from the nose of the plane. A reserve. A private reserve. Just in case.

There is a good deal of squabbling over the roast cat. The pilot, Andrea and the professor seem to wind up with the largest portions. Mine is among the smallest. Off in the black bank of the jungle we can hear the pariah gnashing his teeth, keening. He is taking it hard. The pilot says that he is a

troublemaker anyway and that the community is better off
without him. As I tear into Joy Boy's plump drumstick, I
cannot help agreeing.

Night

Wispy flames tremble at the wicks of three thin birthday
candles Andrea has found in the galley. Their light is sufficient
for the professor. He is tinkering with the radio, and with the
plane's massive battery. Suddenly the cracked speaker comes
to life, sputters, coughs up a ball of static sizzling like bacon in
a frying pan. The pilot is a madman. He bowls over Tanqueray, flings himself on his knees before the radio (think of
altar and neophyte), snatches up the microphone and with
quaking fingers switches to TRANSMIT. "Mayday, Mayday!"
he shouts, "Mayday, Mayday, Mayday."

We freeze—a sound is coming back through the speaker.
The professor tunes it in, the interference like a siren coming
closer and then shooting off in the distance as the sound
clears. It is music, a tune. Tinny mandolins, a human voice—
singing. We listen, rapt, suddenly and magically in communion with the civilized world. The song ends. Then the first
strains of a commercial jingle, familiar as our mothers' faces,
things go better with Coke, but there's something wrong, the
words in a muddle. The announcer's voice comes over—in
Japanese. Radio Tokyo. Then the box goes dead. There is the
smell of scorched wire, melted transistor. The pilot's jaw lists,
tears start in his eyes, his knuckles whiten over the microphone. "Good morning, Mr. Yones," says the professor.
"How are your wife?"

Morning

Many things to report:
1) The tools have vanished. The cat man suspected. Ven-

geance the motive. The pilot and the professor are off in the shadows, hunting him.

2) Tanqueray and the English/allergic man (nose clogged, eyes like open sores) have volunteered to make their way back to civilization and send succor. They are not actuated by blind heroism. The one has finished the miniatures, the other is out of epinephrine. Their chances—a drunken old man and a flabby asthmatic—are negligible. I will not miss them in any case. They are both consummate asses.

3) The mime has begun our constitution. He sits hunched in his seat, face in pancake, looking uncannily like Bernardo O'Higgins.

4) I have made overtures to Andrea. When the pilot and the professor slipped off after the cat man, I took her aside and showed her a tin of sardines. She followed me out of the plane and through the dripping fronds and big squamate leaves. We crouched in the bush. "I had this tucked away in my suitcase," I whispered, lying. "Thought you might want to share it with me—"

She looked at me—the green of her eyes, the leafy backdrop. Her uniform had degenerated to shorts and halter, crudely knotted. Her cleavage was deep as the jungle. "Sure," she said.

"—for a consideration . . ."

"Sure."

I turned the key. The sardines were silver, the oil gold. I counted them out, half for her, half for me. We ate. She sucked her fingers, licked the corners of the tin. I watched her tongue. When she finished she looked up at me, a fat bubble of oil on her lip. "You know," she said, "you're a shit. I mean you're a real shit. Holding out, trying to bribe me. You think I'd do it with you? Listen. You nauseate me with your skinny legs and your filthy beard and your dirty little habits—I've been watching you since you got on the plane back at

Rio. Think I don't know your type? Ha. You're a real shit."

What could I say? We stood. I answered her with the vilest string of expletives I could dredge up (nineteen words in all). She caught me off balance, I tumbled back into the bushes, sat studying the shift of her buttocks as she stalked off. A spider the size of a three-egg omelet darted down the neck of my shirt. I crushed him against my chest, but his bite was like an injection of fire.

Afternoon

"Been holding out on us, eh?"

"Look, I just had the one tin—you can search through my bags if you don't believe me. Go ahead."

"Damn straight I will. And I got a good mind to send you down the road with that freak-faced cat fancier too. You're sure as hell no part of this society, buddy. You never say a damn word, you don't toe your line, and now you're sequestering food . . . You sure there's no more of it?"

"No, I swear it. I just picked up the one tin at Rio—the label caught my eye in the snack shop at the airport."

The pilot's eyes are razors, his jaw a saber. He thrusts, I parry. He paws through my things, sniffs at my sport shirts, pockets a bottle of after-shave. The big fist spasmodically clenches and slackens, bunching the collar of my shirt. The professor looks on, distant, serene. The mime is busy with his writing. Andrea stands in the background, arms crossed, a tight snake's smile on her lips.

Evening

Trees have fallen on trees here in the rain forest. *Mauritia*, orbyguia, *Euterpe*, their branches meshed with wild growths of orchids, ferns and pipers. Stands of palm. The colossal ceibas, Para nuts and sucupiras with their blue flowers high in the sun. I am feeling it, the rain forest, here in the gloom below. Sniffing it, breathing it. In the branches, tail-swinging monkeys and birds of every stripe; in the mold at my feet, two tiny armadillos, tough and black as leather. They root round my shoes, stupid piglike ratlike things. I bend toward them, a drooping statue, slow as the waning sun. My hand hangs over them. They root, oblivious.

I strike.

The big one squeals (faint as a baby smothering in the night), and the smaller scuttles off, more ratlike by the second. Suddenly I am stamping, the blood pounding in my thighs, my shoes like hammers. And then I am sitting in the wet, the spiderbite swelling like a nectarine under my skin, mosquitoes black on my neck, my face, my arms, the strange crushed thing at my feet. I want to tear it, eat it raw, alone and greedy.

But I will take it back, an offering for Andrea's cold eyes and the pilot's terrible jaw. I will placate them, stay with the ship and the chance of rescue—I will shrink, and wait my chance, sly and watchful as a coiled bushmaster.

Night

I am excited, brimming with expectation—and yet stricken with fear, uncertainty, morbid presentiment. I have seen something in the bush—two eyes, a shadow, the hint of a human form. It was not the cat man, not the English/allergic man, not Tanqueray. I have said nothing to the others.

Tonight there are just three of us in the familiar dormitory: the professor, the mime, myself. A single stumpy candle gutters. The door has already closed on the pilot and Andrea. Outside, the leaves rattle with the calls of a thousand strange creatures, cooing, chattering, hissing, clucking, stirring wings, stretching toes, creeping beneath and scrabbling over: a festering backdrop for those pathogenic eyes in the bush.

Morning

Andrea, in bad humor, portions out breakfast—leg of armadillo, (charred scale, black claw), imitation roquefort dressing, a half-ration of water and sour mix. Apiece. She holds back the tail for herself. The mime, in tights and pancake, entertains us with animal impressions: walrus, swan, earthworm. Then he does a man shaving and showering in a flurry of interruptions: the phone, the doorbell, the oven timer. The professor laughs, a weird silent Scandinavian laugh. The pilot and Andrea scowl. My face is neutral.

Suddenly the pilot stands, cutting the performance short. "I've got an announcement," he says. "We might as well face it—this crate'll never fly, no matter how heroic the effort on the part of the prof and me." He hangs his head (think of Christ, nailed to the cross, neck muscles gone loose, his moment of doubt and pain)—but then suddenly he snaps to attention and glares at us, his eyes like the barrels of a shotgun. "And you want to know the reason?" (He is shouting.) "A cut-and-dried case of desertion, that's the reason. Plumface goes and disrupts the community, lets us all down—and then, as if that wasn't enough, he makes off with our tools out of sheer spite. . . . I'm not going to kid you: it looks pretty grim." (Christ again.) "Still, if we stick together—" (here he pauses, the catchword on all our lips) "—we'll lick this jungle yet.

"Now listen. Rummy and Sneezes have been gone for nearly twenty-four hours now. Anytime we could hear those choppers coming for us. So let's get out and clear 'em a landing strip, back to back, like a real community!" Andrea applauds. I seethe. The mime looks like a cross between the unknown soldier and Charles de Gaulle. The professor works his mouth, searching for a phrase.

Outside, just beyond the tail of the plane, is a patch of partially cleared ground, a consequence of the crash. In the center of this patch—undiscovered as yet by any of us—are two freshly cut stakes, set in the ground. On the tips of the stakes, like twin balls of flies or swarms of bees, the heads of Tanqueray and the English/allergic man, dripping.

Afternoon

A quickening series of events:

——The Discovery. The professor faint, Andrea tough as a kibbutz woman.

——The Discussion. The pilot, our leader, punches our shoulders in turn. Slaps our backs. He has decided to abandon the plane in the morning. We will walk back to civilization. In charade, the mime asks if we will not all be decapitated during the coming night, our blood quaffed, bones gnawed by autochthonous cannibals. The pilot steps into his cabin, returns a moment later with a pistol the size of a football. For hijackers, he explains.

——The Preparation. We pull down the life preservers (a rain of scorpions and spiders, birds' nests, strange black hairs). They are the color of the rain slickers worn by traffic patrolmen. We will each wear one, insurance against bottomless swamps and angry copper rivers. In addition, we are each provided with a crude walking stick cum club, at one end of which we tie up our belongings, hobo-fashion. The provisions are slim: we divide up nine individual packets of sugar, six of ketchup, three rippled pepper shakers. Each of us takes a plastic spoon, knife and fork, sealed in polyethylene with a clean white napkin.

——The Plan. We will live off the land. Eat beetle, leech, toad. We will stick together. Walk back. A team.

Evening

The mime has fallen sick. What could it be but the dreaded jungle fever? He writhes in his seat, raves (in pantomime), sweats. His makeup is a mess. The professor tends him, patting his head and crooning softly in Norwegian. Andrea and the pilot keep their distance. As do I.

We do not eat. We will need what little we have for the road. Still, around dinnertime, the pilot and Andrea mew themselves up in his cabin: they have their secrets I suppose. I have my secrets as well. As the cabin door eases shut I slip out into the penumbra of the forest floor, ferret through the stalks and creepers, dig up my hoard (the seven shiny survivors) and silently turn the key on a tin of baby smoked oysters. I pack the rest among my underwear in the tight little bundle I will carry with me in the morning.

Later, we discuss the mime's condition. He is in no shape to travel, and yet it is clear that we cannot remain where we are. In fact, all of us are in a bug-eyed rage to get away from those rotting heads and those terrible shadows and eyes, eyes and shadows. And so, we discuss. No one mentions community, nor refers to the group constitution. The pilot puts it to a vote: stay or leave. Mime or no mime. He and Andrea vote to leave at dawn, regardless of the mime's condition. If he can accompany us, fine. If not, he will have to stay behind (until we can direct a rescue party to the plane of course). I do not want to stay behind. I do not want to carry the mime. I raise my hand. And the professor makes it unanimous, though I doubt if he has any conception of what the vote involves. Aside, he asks me if I can direct him to the library.

Night

Andrea and the pilot choose to sleep in the main cabin for the first time.

We keep a bonfire burning through the darkness.

We share sentry duty.

The sounds of the jungle are knives punched through our chests.

Morning

I wake in a sweat. Everything still. Andrea, all leg, shoulder, navel and cleavage, is snoring, her breath grating like bark stripped from a tree. Beside her, the pilot: captain's cap pulled over his face, gun tucked in his belt. The professor, who had the last watch, is curled in his chair asleep. Outside, the fire has burned to fine white ash and a coatimundi steals across the clearing. Something is wrong—I feel it like a bad dream that refuses to end. Then I glance over at the mime. He looks exactly like John F. Kennedy lying in state. Dead.

There is no time for ceremony. No time in fact for burial. The pilot, sour with sleep, drops a blanket over the frozen white face and leads us cautiously out of the plane, and into the bush. We shoulder our clubs, the white bundles. Our life jackets glow in the seeping gloom. The pilot, Andrea, the professor, me. A team. Pass the baton and run, I think, and chuckle to myself. My expectation of survival is low, but I follow anyway, and watch, and hope, and wait.

We walk for three hours, slimed in sweat, struggling through the leaves, creepers, tendrils, vines, shoots, stems and stalks, over the colossal rotting trunks, into the slick algae-choked ponds. Birds and monkeys screeching in the trees. Agoutis stumbling off at our feet. Snakes. The trails of ants. And in the festering water, a tapir, big as a pregnant horse. I develop a terrible thirst (the pilot, of course, is custodian of our water supply). My throat is sore, lips gummed. I think of the stories I have heard—thirst-crazed explorers plunging their heads into those scummy pools, drinking deep of every foul and crippling disease known to man. And I think of the six shiny tins in my pack.

Suddenly we are stopping (halftime, I suppose). The pilot consults his compass, the great jaw working. Andrea, 97 percent exposed flesh, is like a first-aid dummy. Slashes, paper cuts, welts, sweet droplets of blood, a leech or two, insects spotting her skin like a terminal case of moles. We throw ourselves down in the wet, breathing hard. Things of the forest floor instantly dart up our pantlegs, down our collars. Andrea asks the pilot if he has the vaguest fucking idea of where we're headed.

He frowns down at the compass.

She asks again.

He curses.

She holds up her middle finger.

The pilot takes a step toward her, lip curled back, when suddenly his expression goes soft. There is a look of surprise, of profound perplexity on his face, as if he'd just swallowed an ice cube. In his neck, a dart. A tiny thing, with feathers (picture a fishing lure pinned beneath his chin like a miniature bow tie). And then from the bushes, a sound like a hundred bums spitting in the gutter. Two more darts appear in the pilot's neck, a fourth and fifth in his chest. He begins to giggle as if it were a great joke, then falls to his knees, tongue caught between his teeth. We watch, horror-struck. His eyes glaze, the arms twitch at his sides, the giggles rising like a wave, cresting higher, curling, and then breaking—he drops like a piece of flotsam, face down in the mulch.

We panic. The professor screams. Andrea snatches the
pilot's pistol and begins laying waste to the vegetation. I
stretch out flat, secrete my head, wishing I had a blanket to
pull over it. A random bullet sprays mud and leaf in my hair.
The professor screams again. Andrea has shot him. In the eye.
When I look up, the revolver is in her lap and she is fumbling
with the magazine. There is a dart in her cheek. It is no time
to lose consciousness. But I do.

Afternoon

I wake to the sound of human voices, the smell of smoke. I
lie still, a wax doll, though something tears persistently at the
spider-welt on my chest. My eye winks open: there is a
campfire, nine or ten naked men squatting round it, eating.
Gnawing at bones. Their skin is the color of stained walnut,
their bodies lean as raw muscle, their lips distended with
wooden disks. Each has a red band painted across his face at
eye level, from the brow to the bridge of the nose, like a party
mask. There is no trace of my late teammates.

I find I am suffering from anxiety, the image of the fly-
blackened heads screeching through my mind like a flight of
carrion birds, the quick dark voices and the sound of tooth on
bone grating in my ears. I am on the verge of bolting. But at
that moment I become aware of a new figure in the group—
pasty white skin, red boils and blotches, a fallen, purplish
mask. The cat man. Naked and flabby. His penis wrapped in
bark, pubic hair plucked. I sit up. And suddenly the whole
assembly is on its feet, fingers twitching at bowstrings and
blowguns. The cat man motions with his hand and the
weapons drop. Barefooted, he hobbles over to me, and the
others turn back to their meal. "How you feeling?" he says,
squatting beside me.

I crush an insect against my chest, rake my nails over the throbbing spiderwelt. I opt for sincerity. "Like a piece of shit."

He looks hard at me, deciding something. A fat fluffy tabby scampers across the clearing, begins rubbing itself against his thigh. I recognize Egmont. He strokes it, working his finger under the ribbon round its neck. "Don't ask any questions," he says. And then: "Listen: I've decided to help you—you were the only one who loved my little beauties, the only one who never meant us any harm . . ."

Evening

The last. It is nothing. I follow the brown back of my guide through the shadowy maze, always steering away from the swamps and tangles, sticking to high ground. The cat man has elected to stay behind, gone feral (once an ass, always an ass). Soured on civilization, he says, by his late experience. We have had a long talk. He whimpered and sputtered. Told me of his childhood, his morbid sensitivity—marked at birth, an outcast. He's suffered all his life, and the experience with the downed plane brought it all home. The Txukahameis (that was his name for them) were different. Noble savages. They found him wandering, took him in, marveled over the beauty of his face, appointed him demichief, exacted his vengeance for him. There was a lot to like about them, he said. Home cooking. Sexual rites. Pet ocelots. No way he was leaving. But he wished me luck.

And so I follow the brown back. Five or six hours, and then I begin to detect it—faint and distant—the chuff and stutter of a diesel. Bulldozers, two or three of them. We draw closer, the noise swells. Step by step. I can smell the exhaust. Then my guide points in the direction of the blatting engines, parts the fronds, and vanishes.

I hurry for the building road, my blood churning, a smile cracking my lips—yes, I am thinking, the moment I step from the bush I'll be a celebrity. In a month I'll be rich. Talk shows, interviews, newspapers, magazines—a book, a film. (Birds caw, my feet rush, the bulldozers roar.) I can picture the book jacket . . . my face, jungle backdrop . . . title in red . . . *Survivor* I'll call it—or *Alive* . . . no, something with more flair, more gut appeal, something dramatic, something with suffering in it. Something like—*Green Hell.*

Earth, Moon

THE ASTRONAUT'S HOUSE has been visited with a plague. This is how it is:
   things rusting, crumbling, decomposing, the elements laying waste: smoothing corners and quashing angles, sagging the roof, licking the paint from the shingles. Wind and rain, hot and cold. Things are going to wrack. Down in the basement pools of water grow, brooding and dark, and tree roots shatter the walls. Upstairs the floors buckle, wallpaper peels, pipes strain at their joints. The old spayed dog gives birth in the hallway. There are frogs in the toilet. Crickets in the porridge. Bats. Outside the macadam erupts in the street and the wind pulls the wires down. The shrubs burgeon like magic beanstalks.

The Astronaut's wife, not much at gardening or repairs, sits in her room, a white garment in her lap. She ravels by day, unravels by night. Lately her fingernails are grown long as stilettos and her axillary hair thick as moss. Clip though she will, the nails grow back, the hair persists. A film, yellow and green, has begun to creep over her teeth.

Now, the clack of the loom still echoing in her ears, she listens to the sounds of the house: the dry rasp of the wood borers, acid hiss of the flying ants. The nameless rustlings and scurryings in the hallways, the chirrup of tree toads, rusty creak of the woodwork. Something falls in the next room, wood on wood. She catches her breath. Begins chewing at her nails. Just below her, in the dark kitchen, a spider creeps through the fine white crystals of the salt cellar.

2

Two hundred and thirty-nine thousand miles away the Astronaut shoots back the bolts and rolls open the steel door. Then eases himself through the hatch, relaxes his grip on the handrail and drops to the ground. He sinks to his knees in moon dust. Like a goddam ocean of soap powder he thinks. An ashpit. But then: the cameras roll, the microphone crackles in his ear. Folks, he says. Folks it's like a dream. It's magic, like a snowstorm when you're a kid, like a—like a prayer. And then, his organs ticking, the blood pinching fast through artery and vein, he finds himself dancing for the cameras, pirouetting like a Baryshnikov, the plodding boots light as ballet slippers. He springs out over the waste in wide slow-motion bounds, wobbles back on his heels, bumps his hips and spins out a cartwheel. Then he falls to his knees, winded, and giggles inside his space suit. The earth is setting behind his shoulder, a wrinkled blue pea against the deep. He holds up his thumb and sights along it, one eye winked shut: the pea vanishes. And then something very ordinary happens.

Lunch (the Radarange lobster Newburg), begins to churn in
his stomach. A pressure there. Gas. He shifts to let it go. This
is an historic moment he thinks.

3

Shadows linger, cobwebs darken the corners, mold spreads
a black hand across the window. Dust sifts down like sand in
an hourglass, already half an inch deep on her husband's collection of Japanese clock-radios. She thinks of checking the
TV reports but the electricity is out and the tubes are black. A
bird beats at the pane. She looks up from her work, imagining
things.

When she steps downstairs to look for the nail clippers the
pictures are leaning on their hooks, tilting with the house.
She lifts one from the wall to straighten it and starts at the pair
of geckos stuck to the plaster beneath, one atop the other.
Their eyes are like fire. From outside: the whisper of growing
grass. It is already high as a stand of bamboo.

4

He's in his T-shirt, clamping around in his magnetized
shoes, patting his abdomen. He presses his nose to the glass,
moving at incredible speed. And feels as if he's standing still,
the skylab motionless. There isn't a sound. No rush of wind,
nor rumble of engine. Eerie, he thinks. Unnatural. Then he
looks down at the earth, mammoth, the blue and brown quilt
sloping beneath him. He shakes his head, eyes gone wistful,
then turns back to the exercise machine. He works out. The
sweat begins to collect along his collarbone. He's pumping at
the bicycle pedals, envisioning himself on a French track, laps
ahead of the nearest competitor, when he feels himself grow-

ing hard, straining at the crotch of his sweat pants. He listens for the others. They are asleep—both of them—strapped in on their feet like horses in a stable. What the hell? he thinks, and slips the pants down. He begins to pump in time with his legs, breath coming quicker, quicker, counting down, 3-2-1—

He's never seen anything like it: the stuff, big congealed drops of it, lifting off into the air, floating, drifting, playing off the ceiling and the walls, riding high.

5

The Astronaut's Ghia jolts along the pitted road, leaping fissures, dodging power lines. He drives it hard. Makes the tachometer read red all the way home and into the driveway where the thick-leafed plants hiss along the sides of the car. Damn, he thinks, the place has sure gone to pot.

The yard is a jungle, the house a shack. A muddy stream runs down the slope of the drive. When he swings open the car door a swarm of wasps begins orbiting his head. He swipes at them, they avoid his hand. None land, none sting. They merely circle, a cloud round his head, a halo. The sun is like a torch.

Inside, rodents scrabble off at his footsteps, the doorframe leaks sawdust, toucans whistle from the bookshelves. There are cracks in the crystal. He embraces his wife with a stiff back, the wasps widening their orbit to accommodate the second head. When he moves away from her the swarm goes with him. It's been like this since you left, she says.

Out in the garage he sharpens his scythe with long strokes of the file. The swarm whispers like static in his ears. He lays aside the file, takes a deep breath and sprays the house and garden bug killer full into his face. The wasps fall like heavy rain.

6

The work is hot. He lashes at the jungle grass with his shining scythe, the sun caught in the corner of the crescent. At each stroke butterflies light into the air, and toads spring for deeper grass. He chops, chops, chops. Sweating. The sun hot. Chops, and then hesitates, his face suddenly struck with alarm. He looks over his shoulder, running sweat, feeling for the heavy pinions along his back. The waxen wings are melting.

Quetzalcóatl Lite

IT IS NEAR THE END of my search, leads fizzled, blind alleys plumbed, and I am sunning beside a kidney-shaped pool in the courtyard of a small but decently kept hotel in San Buitre. The grass is clipped, there are gardens of cactus, paths of gravel, a clean cement wall eight or ten feet high. The sky is clear to the rim of the ionosphere and clouds drift by like fragments of a dream. During the course of the past few days I've drunk from stagnant puddles, bathed in my own gritty perspiration, bedded down on the floor of the jungle. I was blistered, stung, chafed, sick to my stomach with dysentery and disappointment. . . . And now I'm reclining here, in cultivated seclusion, by the edge of a limpid blue—or rather, algaic green—swimming pool.

But my mind is far from easy. I've been on a quest—a wildgoose chase perhaps—in which I invested as much heart and soul as an army of Percivals, and I have been frustrated.

Duped. The thought sours my stomach. I sit up to take a long
palliative pull at my rum and tonic, and suddenly they're
there—buzzards, eight or nine of them—circling above me as
I have so many times seen them drifting over the flyblown
corpse of some animal on the plain. They seem to be winding
their way down—there's another one—the closest no more
than a hundred feet from the ground. "So this is it," I think.
"I've slipped beyond the pale." My next thought is for my
collection: eternally incomplete. But then a breath of wind
rattles the branches along the wall and a fine flurry of white
feathers drifts over my chest, the pathway, the still surface of
the pool. Beyond the wall there is the shriek—no, the
squawk—of birds, chickens, throttled and plucked. I grin an
ironic grin. The hotel shares a back wall with the local
butcher.

This is the way things are in this country: illusion mas-
querades as reality. Reality is a tear in the veil of Maya. And I
am caught between. But let me begin at the beginning.

I am a collector. I collect not merely as a hobby or pastime,
but as the principal business of my life, as the constellation
and nexus of my being. Some men gamble, drink, challenge
the Atlantic in hot-air balloons. I collect things.

As a boy I collected indiscriminately: bits of chalk, blackened light bulbs, bottle caps, buttons, disposable lighters,
cigar bands, shoelaces, spindles, slugs, cotter pins, washers,
inkless ball-points, bladeless knives, the crusted and petrified
wads of chewing gum that clustered beneath counters and
tabletops like the plague of boils that ravaged my grandfather's face. Objects, things, crafted and sleek, were my obsession: I hoarded and doted over them like some rubber-
lipped jungle chieftain doting over his talismans. As I grew
into maturity, however, my taste became more discerning.
Looking round me I saw that other collectors sought objects

of recognizable value or beauty: paintings, porcelain, first editions. My own collecting, nonselective and utterly without regard to value, was senseless and puerile by comparison. It was clear that I would have to find a more meaningful focus for my passion. But what to collect? Anyone with means could accumulate Greek amphorae or eighteenth-century portraiture—I hungered for the unique, the exceptional, the object of consummate symmetry and beauty, some new form hitherto overlooked by the *monde vieux* of collectors, that I, their Columbus and their Cortés, would deliver in a storm of applause.

It was in this frame of mind that I first encountered Roger Perdoo, the man who was to become my principal benefactor and bitterest rival. We met at an auction of objets d'art in South Kensington, nearly fifteen years ago. I was twenty-two, just down from Yale and shot through with ennui and various other malaises of the spirit. The trip to London and the Continent was a sort of initiation rite for my pocketbook (have I mentioned that my grandfather was a collector too? —he favored railroads and petroleum refineries). For lack of anything better to do I'd just bid on a pair of morris chairs and a portrait by David, and was making out my check when I felt a pressure on my arm. I looked up into a pair of colorless eyes, vacant as the reaches of the universe. Perdoo's eyes. "You don't really want this garbage, do you?" he said, the force of his grip making a fever chart of my signature. He was about thirty, an Englishman, and there was something striking, incongruous—aberrant even—about his face. It wasn't until later in the evening that I realized what it was: the colors of his hair and eyebrows were radically mismatched, as if there had been some zero-hour failure of the genes. His crown, sideburns and twirled mustache were a sort of alley-cat orange, while his eyebrows, which hovered over the pale irises like birds of prey, were black as pitchblende. Much later I learned that he dyed them to achieve this effect. When I asked him why, he was cryptic—said they were like road-signs, single lane ahead, dangerous curve.

I handed the check to the cashier and turned to face this audacious stranger. "No, I don't really want this bric-a-brac"—I laughed—"but what else is there?"

Perdoo grinned like a snake. "I have just the thing," he whispered.

His flat was within walking distance—Cranley Gardens—fashionable then, overrun with Arabs now. Marble steps, lions couchant, cantilevered windows overlooking a private garden. He switched on a tape—lute pieces by Alberto Glori—and then disappeared into the kitchen. I sat back, taking in the high ceilings, skylights, the potted palm and hibiscus, all the while bursting for a glimpse at his collection—to see if he actually had hit upon something unique and inspirational. In my heart I knew I would be disappointed.

He was back in a moment with a tray of canapés and two cans of beer, no glasses. He set them down on the coffee table, loosened his tie, unbuttoned his collar, and began fishing around beneath his shirt as if he were chasing fleas or patting on sun lotion. I began to feel uncomfortable. But then his hand emerged from the shirt with a solid-gold church key, which he apparently wore on a chain round his neck. He inverted the beer cans and punched a pair of triangles in each. The ritualistic behavior struck me as odd—very odd—but we were soon sipping beer and lamenting the dilettantism of London collectors, and the whole thing slipped my mind. We chatted for ten or fifteen minutes, and then, unable to hold back any longer, I asked to see his collection.

He gazed at me steadily, a grin playing on his lips. "You've already examined one of my rarest and most precious pieces."

I looked round the room, blank as a cow. "I have?"

The grin widened, the eyebrows arched. He began to whistle along with Glori.

Then it struck me. I gazed down at the beer can in my hand. The color scheme was black and tan, decorated with an ellipse in which a detailed miniature of Tumulty's Brewery was represented. I'd been drinking a can of the legendary Tumulty's Cream Ale! "You mean—?"

He nodded.

My life began.

During the ensuing years I haunted junkyards, town dumps, recycling centers, picked through trash barrels in the U.S., Canada, and thirteen other countries, dove off the Great Barrier Reef for a trove of Wallaby Ale that had gone down with a club ship during the war, plumbed the debris of burned-out Cambodian villages for traces of a rice beer that came in checkered cans with poptops at both ends. I was relentless. I toured every brewery in the country, posted rewards with distributors, spent countless hours at ball parks, in the deeps of barrooms, over the grills at public campsites, drinking, swapping stories, acquiring trophies and soaking up legends of vanished brews. Brews like Crowfoot, the American Indian beer "aged in birchbark canoes" and closed down by federal tax agents the day it was launched. Or the Boston stout, drunk warm, which blinded thirteen people back in the fifties. What had become of the eight or ten cases of Crowfoot produced in those dawning hours, or the half-million cans of Beantown Stout that had inundated New England before the FDA could recall them? Mysteries—I pursued them with the rigor of a Zen master, the zeal of a private eye on a smut case.

I began to put on weight, my liver ached, but no matter—my collection outstripped Perdoo's inside of three years. He simply didn't have my resources or tenacity. I had crateloads of the conventional pieces and my trophy room boasted

an unblemished copy of every American can produced in the
past four decades, and a significant number of foreign cans as
well—including a scorched and blistered relic of Über-
menschbräu, a Gestapo favorite, and a rare specimen of a
little-known Lapp beer which bore the imprint of an ungulate's hoof.

As the field narrowed, however, the objects of my search
became increasingly exotic. I paid ridiculous sums to obtain
cans of special significance—the first Falstaff can Bob Dylan
had ever held to his lips, a Missouri Mule can found under
Harry Truman's bed, the can of Via Media that John XXIII
had hastily downed before the first convocation of the Ecu-
menical Council. I sought out the "freaks" as well—cans mis-
labeled, misshapen, improperly seamed or stamped, poptops
that wouldn't pop—the hunchbacks and harelips of the bot-
tling industry. Still I wasn't satisfied. I was haunted by
legends of ancient beers, obsessed with rumors of fanciful
brews like the Guatemalan millet beer spiked with psilocybin
or the Ugandan shandy purportedly diluted with blood—human, some said. Voices whispered out of the shadows,
seethed through my dreams, soured my morning coffee. I
couldn't rest till I'd tracked down every last one, confronted
the myths in their lairs, held in my greedy trembling hands
the first and last cans ever produced. I was driven, yearning
for an impossible, unattainable completeness, a cosmic sense
of well-being and return to home—driven until I was led to
undertake this last and fateful expedition into the very mar-
row of the legend itself.

Two weeks ago we landed at San Ibis, a soporific little town
in the foothills. There were four of us: Perdoo, my wife Netti,
Joaquín Spinnaker, and myself. Spinnaker was a graduate
student in archaeology at some university in southern
California, Chicano on his mother's side. We brought him

along as an interpreter and extra hand. Netti was my fourth. She was a brooder, hair in a topknot, eyes like smoke. We'd been married six months.

The expedition was conceived and organized by Perdoo, underwritten by me. Ostensibly we were doing fieldwork on some of the rarer Latin American brews—Pelicano, Belikin, Punta Gorda lager—but our actual purpose lay deeper. We were heading for a new and extensive ruin recently discovered in the jungles of Santa Gallina—a ruin as yet undisturbed by the inevitable hordes of archaeologists, looters, tourists and sociopaths. There, under cover of darkness if necessary, we were bound and determined to screen every square inch of soil for traces of the fabled Quetzalcóatl Lite, brew of the ancient Aztecs.

No, we were not suffering from some group hallucination. All of us, with the possible exception of Spinnaker (perhaps the most uninspired and lethargic human being I've ever encountered), believed or wanted to believe in the existence of Quetzalcóatl Lite. After all, beers have been with us for over eight thousand years—beers of Egypt, Nubia, Ur—beers that Pliny spoke of, that Dante dreamed over, beers that washed the feet of Christ. But what of cans? We've used them for little more than a century and a half now, and the understanding of pasteurization is even more recent than that. Quite right. But you wouldn't think the ancients had flying machines either—or stellar observatories or trigonometry or sculpture that would break Rodin's heart, would you? Man has forged metal for five thousand years now. Who can say for certain to what heights ancient civilization attained? If the Aztecs had paved roads, aqueducts, and temples two hundred feet high, why not so small and vital a thing as a beer can?

We put up overnight at the Hotel Inercia in San Ibis, while Spinnaker arranged for transportation to Santa Gallina in the morning. The hotel was owned and operated by a pair of weathered Arizonans—Skipper and Lulu—who had migrated south to escape the inconvenience of paying city, school, federal, state, sales, refuse and sewer taxes on a fixed income. They were both in their seventies. Skipper suffered from chronic arthritis, and Lulu experienced prolonged periods of confusion. The sheets were clean. Outside in the courtyard stood a thatch of tropical green alive with toucans, lizards and three-inch cockroaches. There was a cold shower downstairs.

At dinner that evening we drank Punta Gorda lager and scraped black beans and white rice from our plates. There was meat too: something Skipper called venison but which Perdoo identified as dog. Netti was in the toilet through most of the meal. Flies settled on her food.

Skipper joined us for dessert (rice pudding) and coffee. The damp weather had inflamed his arthritis, and he found it difficult to manage fork and spoon. Lulu hand-fed him, as if he were an infant. After the first mouthful he loosened up a bit, looked me in the eye and croaked: "So it's beer cans you're after, is it?"

"That's right," Perdoo answered, deadpan.

Skipper turned to Perdoo. "Well I know where you can get a whole shitload of 'em."

"It's not the whole shitload that interests us, my friend," said Perdoo.

Lulu was dreaming. The next installment of pudding landed in Skipper's lap. He glanced up at me with a cagey glint in his eye. "Well maybe it's a can of that Quetzal Lite that'll make you sit up smart, eh?"

I arched my back as if I'd been slapped across the spine with a two-by-four. "You . . . you know of it?"

Lulu laughed. "Does he know of it?" she cackled, inadvertently shoving a spoonful of pudding up Skipper's nose. "Damn it, woman," he hissed, snapping out at her finger. She jerked her hand away and slapped the bowl to the floor. Then stood shakily and trundled out of the room, pausing at the doorway to turn her wizened face to us. "Don't listen to a word he says," she choked. "He's a born liar."

"I can lead you right to it," Skipper insisted, a rice kernel clinging to the side of his nose. "Up Santa Gallina."

Perdoo yawned. "You were there?"

Skipper nodded.

"Did you see the can?"

"Well, no, I didn't see it personally. But I know this in-dian—Nezhuatlcóyotl—he seen it."

"And the design?"

"Quetzal bird, green head, orange below. Blood-red background, legend in hieroglyph."

Perdoo stared down at the table as if he were studying a chess problem. Skipper looked up at him like a dog waiting for scraps. "I'll do it for a hundred," Skipper said finally, the rice kernel slipping down the wing of his nose and coming to rest on his upper lip. He speared it with his tongue.

Roger looked up. "You're on," he said.

It was eight tortuous red-dust hours to Santa Gallina via jeep—or rather, VW bus. Spinnaker had chartered what must have been the first one ever run off the assembly line at Wolfsburg: oozing shocks, a pox of rust, roof and windows gone, body hacked down to form the lip of a sort of mobile tub. Perdoo sat at the big horizontal wheel, silent and inscru-table behind a pair of mirror-lens sunglasses. Skipper navi-gated, muttering directions and spitting bulbs of tobacco juice into the dust, his shoulders pinched forward as if he were wearing a straitjacket. Netti, Spinnaker and I occupied the rear seat. I watched the bright trunks, dark leaves, the blur of creeper and tendril at the side of the road, and saw a rippling vision of my trophy room, the velvet-shrouded shelves backlit with fluorescent tubes, and the vacant spot, already labeled and set aside for the ultimate trophy: Quetzalcóatl Lite. I could taste the excitement in the back of my throat.

Spinnaker, on the other hand, was unperturbed. He puffed away at a striped reefer the size of a cigar, head dipping between the pages of a Spider-Man comic book. Netti was stricken. Every fifteen minutes she made Perdoo stop while she shoved off into the vegetation with a roll of toilet paper. Skipper never failed to bellow "Montezuma's revenge!" at her retreating back, and then collapse in a vermicular spasm, as if this comment were the culmination of thirty centuries of Western wit. After the fourth or fifth time Perdoo said something terse and savage, and Skipper was a whipped dog all over again.

There were no accommodations in Santa Gallina, but for some unaccountable reason there was a tourist office. It was a shack, actually, planks warped and weathered as driftwood. Inside, a table and chair flanked a red Coca-Cola machine stacked with beer, and two travel posters decorated the walls: Visit Santo Pelicano (On the Coast); See the Aztec Ruins. The proprietor was the size of a ten-year-old, barefoot, dark, his hair cut in a thatch. He opened the machine with a key and set five beaded cans of El Grial on the table. Skipper bent from the waist and clutched the lip of a can in his teeth, straightened up, threw his head back and drank off the entire twelve ounces without pausing for air. He let the empty can clatter to the floor. "Una otra," he said. Netti huddled in the chair, unable to touch hers. Spinnaker offered her two of his Lomotil tablets and then began a rapid-fire conversation with the proprietor. Roger looked on, impassive, the silver lenses like a fun-house mirror. I didn't understand a word.

Then an odd thing happened: as I stared at the Aztec poster I found myself drawn into the action it depicted, discovering new details, projecting life into the scene like Keats revolving the urn on its pedestal. There were pyramids fringed by treetops and lianas, a half-naked girl in a gold headdress, a group of astonished or delirious Indians in shorts or skirts. In the foreground, larger in perspective than the pyramids themselves, was a priest of some sort, his face painted, copper bands round his ankles and wrists, a plume of feathers in his hair. He was bleeding a chicken over a wooden bowl—a chicken unplucked and unruffled save for the fact that one side of its neck had been shaved to the bone. The blood fell in droplets shaped like tears.

Roger broke into my reverie to announce that he was going with "this brown gentleman here" to check out an alternate path to the ruins. They would be back in an hour or so, and then we'd start off. It was all right with me: since we'd pulled into town I'd been itching to comb the banks of the river for treasures.

"Think I'll just stroll down by the river and see what I can find while we're waiting," I said. "Who knows? Might even pick up a mint-condition Hidalgo Mandala or a Cerveza Cabera, 1958." I grinned, stuffed the El Grial empties in my pack and stepped out into the sun-blanched streets of Santa Gallina.

The town was nothing: a hill dominated by a church the size of an Exxon station, sixty shacks, a general store, cantina, dirt streets, chickens, pigs, the jungle. Down by the river I poked through heaps of flotsam, stirring up scorpions and wolf spiders, looking for the odd treasure among the debris. There were plastic bottles, soup cans, banana skins—but nothing worth stooping for. The sun slow-cooked the back of my neck, mosquitoes tenderized my ears. Under a bush I found a decapitated doll. Then, up ahead, I spotted a water-run brushpile glinting with points of reflected light. I sloshed up to it and threw back a mantle of leaf and branch: an oil can winked up at me. But then I stopped dead. There, in the heart of the

nest, undulating gently with the wash of the current, was a
dead chicken—unplucked and unruffled save for the fact that
one side of its neck had been shaved to the bone.

When I got back to the tourist office I found it deserted.
Outside where the van had been parked a striped sow lay
snoozing in the dust. I was puzzled, hurt, annoyed. Beginning
to feel feverish. The faces leered at me from the poster: See
the Aztec Ruins. Had they deserted me? It couldn't be. I
helped myself to a beer, and in the process of punching holes
in the roof of the can, thought of the cantina.

The cantina was just up the street, next door to the church.
It consisted of a thatched awning, a bar, five or six tables.
From a distance the aniline flash of our backpacks stood out
like a dab of color on a black and white canvas. The backpacks
lay in a heap just beyond the perimeter of the awning. White
sun, black shade. When I stepped under the thatch I found
Skipper at the bar, a glass of the local rum before him; Netti
and Spinnaker sat at the farthest table, passing a joint. Perdoo—and the van—were gone.

"Where's Roger?" I demanded.

Skipper's T-shirt was brown with dribbled rum. His eyes
were on fire. "He went up the ruins with that little rooster
from the tourist office."

My bowels clenched—as with the onset of Netti's com-
plaint. I leaned over the bar for support. "You mean . . . he's
already up there? Alone?"

Netti and Spinnaker were laughing over something—heads
thrown back, delirious, slapping the table and wheezing for
breath.

"No, he ain't alone," Skipper enunciated. "Like I *told* you,
that little sharper Nezhuatlcóyotl is with him."

Nezhuatlcóyotl! The world was crashing down around my

ears. All at once I began to appreciate Perdoo's motive for inviting me along on this expedition. That son of a bitch. I'd paid for our air fare, the equipment, Spinnaker's salary, the van, meals, hotels. We were acrobats, and I'd stood on the bottom, giving Perdoo leverage to clear the wall.

I grabbed Skipper's arm. "Can you lead us up there—I mean right this minute?"

He looked me in the eye. "Two hundred," he croaked.

Skipper tottered along, out of tilt, through a congeries of leaf, vine, stem and shoot, no path discernible save for the smooth highways of the army ants. I followed close on his heels, overweight, winded, running with sweat, a roll of toilet paper in one hand, my fisherman's knife in the other. Spinnaker and Netti brought up the rear. As we fought our way through the galaxies of insects, leeches and leg biters, I had only one thought in mind: to get to Perdoo before he could lay claim to the one thing in the world that mattered: Quetzalcóatl Lite.

The sun sank in the treetops, the jungle went from green to gray. Birds, monkeys, frogs and insects rattled the branches and screeched. I asked Skipper if he knew where he was going and he grunted in the affirmative, but the next moment he pitched headfirst down an embankment and into a scummy pool boiling with saurian life. He boiled along with it until Spinnaker fished him out. Then he stood on the bank and cursed consecutively and persistently for two or three minutes, ending in a tearful admission that he hadn't the vaguest notion of where we were. It was now nearly dark, the big jagged leaves of the rain forest receding into blackness at five or six feet. I was incensed. Spinnaker suggested camping where we were—"I mean at least we got water here," he pointed out. But then something remarkable happened: Netti spotted a light through the trees and up the rise to our left. We headed toward it, barking shins and twisting ankles all the way.

When we got close, the light died. Skipper hallooed, and Spinnaker apparently followed suit in Spanish. There was no answer. We broke out our flashlights and followed the rise up to a rocky crest tangled with creeper and bush. As far as any of us could tell, the place was deserted. "I know I saw a light," Netti said. "Me too," said Spinnaker. Skipper staggered up, shoes sloshing, and threw himself down on the rocky pinnacle. Mosquitoes the size of dragonflies settled on us and Skipper began to complain of injuries suffered in his fall. "It's no joke," he moaned, "—think I might of busted something in my sacroiliac."

At that moment a bone-blistering shriek started up from the darkness and a light flashed in the bush twenty feet off. Spinnaker leaped up shouting, Netti became tangled in the straps of her backpack, my flashlight dropped to the ground. A face, red and hideous, leered at us out of the light. We were stunned and confused—but the confusion was short-lived. It was Perdoo. He was holding a flashlight under his chin like a teenaged wiseguy, a Mephistophelean grimace on his face. And then he was laughing, the fierce black eyebrows arching like a clown's. Nezhuatlcóyotl stood at his side. Grinning.

"You sneaking, son-of-a-bitching, backstabbing opportunist!" I shrieked, shaking the toilet paper at him in rage and confusion. "First you sucker me into flying you out here, then you run off with the van, desert me in Dysentery City and sneak out into the jungle to beat me to the find."

He denied it all. Claimed he and Nez were investigating the possibilities of the shortcut when they got lost and found themselves at the ruins, torn between going back for us or beginning the dig. Since darkness was setting in they decided

to spend the night and then go for the rest of us in the morning. He was a poor liar. I demanded to see the dig.

"Down there," he said, pointing over Skipper's shoulder. I
stood on the outcrop and looked down. It was difficult at first,
especially considering the dim tubes of illumination thrown
by the flashlights, but then it came to me: we were atop the
temple itself!

Perdoo chuckled behind me.

What came next wasn't all that pretty. Over the objections
of the entire party, I insisted on hiking down to the dig and
setting to work. They followed reluctantly. When we got to
the base of the pyramid I saw that Perdoo had staked out an
area perhaps five feet square and flush with the lower steps of
a stairway, now mantled with soil and undergrowth, which
presumably ran uphill to the crest of the pyramid. He'd
hardly scratched the surface. I hung my Coleman lantern on a
tree branch, crushed a scorpion or two, and began attacking a
barely perceptible hummock with spoon and scalpel. Skipper
settled down to watch, while Netti and Spinnaker moved off
to set up camp. Perdoo and the Indian stood behind me, their
arms folded.

Half an hour later Skipper was dozing, Perdoo and the
Indian had disappeared, and the odor of dehydrated
stroganoff and swamp water hung on the night air. Bats
coasted through the light, animals cried in the shadows. My
back ached, but I kept at it. Staring down at the blank red
earth my eyes filled with the image of Quetzalcóatl Lite—
riding the air like the Grail—till I could see nothing else.
Then I hit paydirt. The scalpel struck an object, perhaps
metal, an inch and a half down. I broke the crust, chipped and
swept until I unearthed a tin-plated rim that looked like—it
was!—the lip of a beer can. At that moment Skipper woke.

"You find something?" he asked, getting to his feet. My heart raced. I chipped, scraped and brushed with a trembling hand. "I think so," I said.

"Yahoo!" Skipper hollered, dancing round me. "He's got something!" he shouted. "Eureka!" A moment later Netti and Spinnaker were standing over me, eyes wide. "You really on to something?" Spinnaker said. "What is it honey?" Netti chimed.

It was a beer can, half unearthed, but too rusted to make a positive identification as yet. "Get back!" I shouted, but Spinnaker was already grabbing for it. The scalpel punctured his hand and then we were rolling on the ground, punching and flailing, while Skipper kicked at the can with the toe of his boot and Netti scrambled for it like a halfback after a fumble. There was no social contract, no world of Ford Foundations, United Ways and brotherhood of man, no church, state or family—there was only a can in the ground, there was only treasure. We fought over it like the cormorants we were. Unfortunately Spinnaker was more cormorant than I. He was also considerably stronger. He struck me twice in the face and then sprang up to tackle Skipper, who had pried the thing loose and was dribbling it off into the shadows, soccer-style. Skipper fell on the can, pinning it beneath his torso. Spinnaker and Netti fell atop Skipper.

When I heaved up from the bushes, panting, and crazed as a baited bear, Spinnaker was standing in the circle of light, the can in one hand, a nasty-looking cudgel in the other. Netti stood behind him. It was a revelation. "So," I bellowed, "that's how it is," already feeling along my belt for the fishing knife. I was six years old, out on the playground, bullied and betrayed, the cap or ball dangling before my nose. I was beyond reason. Spinnaker stepped toward me. "I'm gonna rip your pig face off!" he shouted. The knife, with its serrated scaler, was in my hand. It was a scene from a thousand movies.

But then suddenly the shriek of a whistle, loud as a back-burning jet, split the night. It was Perdoo. "What the hell's going on here? Some kind of morality play?" Spinnaker retreated a step, dropping the can. I lowered my knife. Perdoo stepped into the glare of the lantern like an actor taking a curtain call, stooped for the can and raised it to the light. Skipper lay on the ground, sniveling. Nezhuatlcóyotl watched from the shadows. Perdoo was grinning. The lower section of the can, relatively free from corrosion, was plainly visible. I recognized the red stripe immediately. It was a Budweiser can.

My personal catharsis came hard on the heels of this revelation, and I stole off into the bushes with the roll of toilet paper, more precious to me at that moment than a truckload of antiquities. I was sick in soul and body: disappointed, deserted, humiliated. And my insides were on fire. Perdoo came to me later, his voice a tranquilizer, commanding and concerned. He had a cup of tea for me, brewed from native herbs. "Drink it," he said. "It'll soothe your stomach."

I woke in a panic to the chemical glow of the tent's walls. An insect, composed entirely of head and pincers, was savaging the back of my neck. My watch read five past two. I leaped up, cursing Perdoo and his tea, and ran for the dig. The sun, strained through the colander of the forest, pierced the gloom with long tapering spotlights. Off in the trees parrots and macaws were having a good laugh over something. My legs pumped, chest heaved. I was frantic, seething with paranoia, certain they'd made a dozen finds without me—but I was surprised. The dig was deserted, and untouched save for the displaced Budweiser can. I cupped my hands and shouted, but there was no response. Then I turned back to the campsite—and realized with a shock that my tent stood alone in the clearing. I was stupefied. I'd been beaten, drugged, conspired against and now deserted in the midst of a tropical rain forest. But to what end? I was soon to find out.

Back at camp I took a fistful of pills to combat gastric pains and a Hershey bar for energy, then hurried off to explore the rest of the site, more than ever convinced of the existence of Quetzalcóatl Lite. No more than five hundred yards off I came upon what appeared to have been a central plaza, now shaded by colossal sucupiras and cluttered with fallen trunks the size of oil rigs. A number of leaf- and tree-choked hummocks were set round the perimeter of this open space, suggesting one- and two-story buildings inundated by the centuries. At the first of these I came across a deep and extensive dig. The ground was littered with shards of polychrome masks and vessels of baked clay, with stone tools and fragments of jade figurines. The earth was soft, freshly sifted. In a deep recess beneath a carved stela I found two suspicious impressions in the earth. Each was precisely the size and shape of a beer can. In the second of these I discovered a metal object—gold, in fact. It was the church key that Perdoo had worn round his neck.

As I stood there, knee-deep in the rubble of this stripped and ravaged tomb, twisting Perdoo's gold in my hands, I gradually became aware that I was not alone. I looked up— into the black bristle mustaches of six members of the Policía Nacional. One of them stepped forward, snatched the church key from my hand, and cuffed my wrists together. Another kicked me in the groin.

And so, here I am in San Buitre, licking my wounds under a sky spotted with carrion birds and rubbed clean again with the down of slaughtered chickens. It's fitting in a way: the hens and pullets are not the only ones to have taken a plucking.

The Policía Nacional showed depths of compassion after I carpeted the station house in traveler's checks and the odd pink and brown bills they use for money in this corner of the world. I remain, however, under a sort of house arrest until some determination can be made regarding the looted objets d'art. The article in the London *Times* did describe Perdoo's remarkable and priceless finds—an obsidian drinking vessel in the form of a gamecock and an alabaster vase representing the rain god Tlaloc, among others—but made no mention of Quetzalcóatl Lite. I begin to wonder if the whole thing wasn't an elaborate Perdoovian hoax designed to induce me to finance his depredations.

Netti, apparently, is alive and well. In the midst of a flurry of bills from airlines and rent-a-car companies, I received a letter from her lawyer. She wants the house in Laguna Beach, half the value of my collection and three million dollars. She also says she wants a life with Spinnaker. Why not? There will be others.

What disturbs me most about this calamitous expedition, however, is not that I've been swindled by Perdoo and deserted by my wife, but that it forces a reappraisal of values on my part. I have given my life over to an anal, exclusive and narcissistic activity, a paradigm of misplaced values that breeds the sort of viciousness and alienation I've suffered in the past weeks. I am a collector. Of cans. Empty cans. The metaphor is so blatant and damning I need not bore you with an exegesis. I've come to understand all this, and at times I think only of flying home, loading the whole cursed collection into the back of a pickup truck and rushing it to the nearest recycling center.

But then I weaken. Picturing those precise and sculpted

forms, backlit against a field of black velvet, their colors aglow, the rich dark calligraphy of the slogans like formulas of the cabbala. Refuse, garbage, junk—lost forever but for daring and innovative collectors like myself and a few cognoscenti like Johns and Warhol. I weaken. And reread the last few lines of a letter from Perdoo, conciliatory and apologetic, lines that make reference to a strange and wonderful new beer he's heard rumor of—I give it no credence of course, and yet the notion intrigues me. A Himalayan beer, brewed and bottled by the Sherpas themselves. They call it Yeti.

De Rerum Natura

THE INVENTOR is in his laboratory, white smock, surgical mask, running afoul of the laws of nature. Schlaver and Una Moss are with him, bent over the Petri dishes and dissecting pans like conspirators. Overhead, the hum of the fluorescent lights.

He snaps his hands into the rubber gloves, flashes the scalpel. His touch is quick, sure, steady as a laser. The blade eases through the shaved skin of the abdomen, his fingers flutter, vessels are clamped, ligatures tied. Una is there, assisting with sponges and retractors. The Inventor's eyes burn over the mask like the eyes of an Arab terrorist. A single sweatpearl stands on his forehead. Strapped to the table before him, teats sleepy with milk, irises sinking, the sedated sow gargles through her crusted nostrils, stirs a bristling hock. Una pats the pink hoof.

Then he is speaking, the tones measured, smooth, the

phrases clipped. Schlaver moves in, draws off the amniotic fluid. Una takes the forceps, offers the scalpel. The Inventor slits the sack, reaches in, pulls his prize from the steaming organs. He slaps the wet nates: the wrinkled little creature shrieks, and then again, its electric wail poking into mason jars, behind filing cabinets, rattling the loose screws in the overhead lights. Una and Schlaver tear off their masks and cheer. The Inventor hefts his latest coup, a nine-pound-three-ounce boy, red as a ham and perfect in every detail: his firstborn, son and heir. The black eyes grin above the mask.

from *The Life*

To say merely that he was a prodigy would mock the insufficiency of language. At five he was teaching in the temple. By age seven he had built his first neutron smasher, developed a gnat-sized bugging device that could pick up a whispered conversation at two miles and simultaneously translate it into any one of thirteen languages, and devised a sap-charging system which fomented rapid growth in deciduous trees of the temperate zone.* At nine he was admitted to MIT, where he completed advanced degrees in physics and mathematics prior to his thirteenth year. During the course of the next eleven months he studied surgical medicine at Johns Hopkins.

At fifteen he stunned the world with his first great advance, the stoolless cat, which brought him the financial independence to sustain his subtler and more meaningful future work. Through an accelerated but painstaking process of selective breeding he had overseen the evolution of a strain of common housecat—the usual attributes intact—which never in the course of its normal lifespan was actuated by the physiological

---

*The oaks and willows shadowing the home of Helmut Holtz, his first tutor, have attained heights in excess of three hundred feet, and continue to grow at an annual rate of nine feet, three and three quarters inches.

demands of micturition or defecation. Within six months after its introduction the major producers of cat litter had thrown in the towel and pet shops were opening next to every liquor store in the country. His photograph (contemplative, the horn-rims) appeared on the covers of Newsweek *and* Time *during the same week. He was hailed. "An Edison for the Seventies," "The Pragmatist's Einstein," they said. Housewives clamored. The Russians awarded him the Star of Novgorod. Encouraged, he went on to develop the limbless, headless, tailless strain that has since become an international institution. A tribute to his disinterestedness: "Under no circumstance, no matter how attractive the inducement," he said, "will I be persuaded to breed out the very minimal essence of the feline—I refer to its purr."**

He is in his study, musing over the morning's mail. The mail, corners, edges, inks and stamps like the tails of tropical birds, lies across his desk in a welter. In his hand, the paper knife. He selects an envelope printed in a blue and yellow daisy pattern.

It is a threat.

Next he picks up a business envelope, imprinted with the name and logo (an ascending rocket) of his son's school: WERNHER VON BRAUN ELEMENTARY SCHOOL. It is a letter from his son's teacher. She is alarmed at what appears to be a worsening deformity of the boy's feet (so misshapen as almost to resemble hoofs, she says) and hopes that his father will have the matter looked into. She is also concerned with his behavior. The boy has, it seems, been making disruptive noises

---

*In Finland, for example, a 10.3 annual per capita consumption of the Furballs (pat. trade name) is indicated. At Reykjavik they are sold on the street corner. An American Porno Queen posed nude in a sea of Furballs for a still-controversial spread in a men's publication. And the Soviet Premier has forgone bedclothes for them. His explanation: "Can you make to purr the electric blanket?"

in the classroom. A sort of whinnying or chuffing. The Inventor carefully folds the letter, tucks it into the pocket of his shirt. At that moment the double doors yawn and Una Moss, in deshabille, ambles in behind the tea cart. Her pet python, weaving a turgid S in the rug behind her, stops at the door.

She pours the Inventor's tea (two lumps) while he frowns at the mail. As she turns to leave, he speaks. "Una?" She looks, puckers a moue. "What is this business with the boy? It seems he's been emitting those noises in the schoolroom." Una's expression irons to the serious. "We can't have that," he says. "Will you speak with him?"

"Of course, pumpkin."

He looks down again. The door closes behind Una, a gentle click, and he turns back to the mail. A brown-paper parcel catches his eye. The paper knife makes a neat incision and he extracts the contents: a hard-cover book. No letter, no inscription. *The Island of Dr. Moreau* by H. G. Wells. He folds back the page, begins to read.

from *The Life*

His second major breakthrough was also a humanitarian effort. A committee from the Gandhi foundation had come to him asking for a solution to the problem of world hunger. He told them he would consider their petition, though engaged in other projects at the time. That afternoon, while rooting through a local wrecking yard in search of a tailpipe replacement for his automobile, the solution rushed on him like a fire storm. "Of course," he was heard to mutter. He retraced his steps to the proprietor's blistered shed. There he borrowed a #2 faucet wrench, ball peen hammer and screwdriver. He then removed the tailpipe from a sandwiched auto of identical make and model to his own. This involved twelve minutes, thirty-seven seconds, as near as investigators have been able

*to determine. In the short space of this time he had worked out
the complicated structural formulae which resulted in one of
mankind's biggest boons—that is to say, he discovered the
method by which a given tonnage of spotted chrome and
rusted steel could be converted to an equivalent weight of
porterhouse steak.*

He is at Horn & Hardart, surrounded by strangers. The boy
sits across from him, head down, heels swinging, fingers
fluffed with the meringue from his third slice of pie. Una's
handbag perches like a sentinel at the edge of the table. Suddenly the boy begins to grunt: hurp-hurp-hurp. The Inventor
looks uncomfortable. He raises a finger to his lips—but the
grunting cracks an octave and the boy pins the plate to the
table, begins licking. The Inventor remonstrates. The plate
rattles on the Formica. Heads turn. The Inventor stands,
looking for Una. Then strides to the bank of tiny windows and
stainless steel doors, fishing in his pocket for coins. Behind
him the grunting increases in volume. He peers into each
window until he finds a slice of lemon meringue pie, yellow
sliver, brown peaks. He puts the coins in the slot, tugs at the
door. It does not open. He tugs harder, taps at the glass, tries
another coin. There is the slap of the boy's plate on the tiles,
and then his angry wail. A middle-aged woman, a stranger, is
trying to comfort him. The Inventor's armpits are moist. He
jerks at the door, tries to spring it with his penknife. The
howls at his back, the ripe flush of the woman's face. And
then, from the Ladies' Room, Una. Like a savior. Green
eyeshade, black caftan, copper anklets.

from *The Life*

*The Inventor's marriage with Roxanne Needelman was
never consummated. She was twenty-nine, a laboratory as-*

sistant, twice married and widowed. He was eighteen, raw, ingenuous, in the first flush of his monumental success with the stoolless cat. After a disastrous honeymoon at Olduvai Gorge the two set up separate households. Three years later the marriage was terminated. The Inventor, immersed in his work, retired to his estate in northern Westchester.

During the course of the next five years he lived and worked alone, perfecting the Autochef and laying the theoretical groundwork for expanding the minute. On the eve of his twenty-sixth birthday he began his association with Yehudi Schlaver, the German-born physicist who would be with him to the end. Two years later, on a rainy April evening, the front buzzer sounded through the umbrageous corridors of the Westchester mansion. At the door, Una Moss. She was wearing a backpack. Two tote bags lay at her feet. She had followed the Great Man's career, saved the clippings from over fifty periodicals, and now she had come to live with him. The Inventor stood in the doorway, his brow square as the spine of a book. He pushed open the door.

Una, Schlaver, the Inventor, his son. They stand at the rail of the Dayliner, in identical London Fog overcoats. On their way to Bear Mountain, for an outing. The air like bad breath, sky black, the water thick and dun-colored. An amateur photographer, passing in a small craft, recognizes the celebrated faces and takes a snapshot: Una, eyes shaded in purple, the rock python wrapped under her chin like primordial jewelry and disappearing in the folds of her overcoat, its head visible beneath the sleeve; Schlaver, small, gray, nondescript; the Great Man, his blocklike brow, the creases like chains running deep into the hairline, the black eyes pinched behind the horn-rims, the point of the beard, lank arms, stooped back; and the boy, feet concealed in custom-built boots, ears already growing to a point and peeping like tongues from beneath the bristling hair. Waves lap, the deck rises, dips. Una, Schlaver and the boy wave. The Inventor hangs his head and disgorges the contents of his stomach.

At the dock, the boy darts ahead, repeatedly stumbling in his boots. Schlaver and Una follow, the one taking charge of the Inventor's compass, calculator and notebooks, the other dragging a picnic basket. The Inventor, sulking, brings up the rear. It begins to drizzle.

A picnic table, prettily reflecting inverted treetops in a sheen of rainwater. The three, collars up, noses dripping, chewing stolidly. In silence. The boy, boots in hand, merrily roots among the wildflowers, nudging at the wet red earth with the bridge of his nose. "Screee-honk-honk," he says, at intervals. The Inventor looks unutterably depressed. He stands, buckles the belt round his raincoat. "Una. I will take a short walk. I wish to be alone, and to be among the trees and mosses." He strides off, into the black bank of pine and beech. Continues on, deep in thought. The trees look alike. He loses his way. When night falls, Una and Schlaver become alarmed. They step into the shadows of the first trees and halloo. There is no answer.

In the morning, search parties are organized. Bloodhounds, state police, boy-scout troops, helicopters, flares. The Governor mobilizes the National Guard. The Vice-President flies in. The voice of the Inventor's mother (a wizened old woman in a babushka) is boomed through enormous loudspeakers. Woodsmen begin felling trees, burning off ground cover. The Inventor has vanished.

Forty days later, Una, who alone has refused to give up the search, is struggling down a slick and rock-strewn slope. Again, rain falls. Again, she wears the overcoat. Again, she accommodates the reptile (the head a comfort in her hand). At the base of the hill, a swamp. Her boots slosh through the clots of algae, heels tug against the suck of the mud. She looks up to flail at a spider web and there he is, squatting naked in a ring of skunk cabbage, his back dancing with mosquito and fly. The glasses are gone, the black eyes crazed and bloodshot. "Here," she says, and holds out her hand. He looks up at her, confused, then slowly lifts his hand to hers, loses his fingers in the triangular black mouth of the snake.

from *The Life*

The now infamous "Bear Mountain Sojourn" marked the decline of the Inventor's practical humanitarian phase. He called a press conference, announced his intention of permanently retiring to his home in suburban Westchester for the purpose of undertaking his great work, a work which would "spiritually edify the race of men as [his] previous work had materially edified them." For seven years nothing was heard of him. Of course there were the usual garbage sifters and mail steamers, the reports from the Inventor's few privileged friends, the speculations of the press. And from time to time paparazzi came up with photographs of the Great Man: brooding on the bedroom fire escape, rooting in the turf with his son, sending up frozen slashes of foam (his slick arm poised) while swimming laps in the pool. Still, he was all but lost to the public eye.

It was during the Seven Years of Silence that a nefarious innovation with enormous market potential appeared briefly in this country and in two Western European nations: a colorless, tasteless liquid, which, when combined with food or drink, reduced the ingestor to a heap of desiccated flakes. When the flakes were moistened, the desiccatee would regain his/her normal structure, totally free of side effects. Abuses of

the product were legion. And though the FDA banned its sale
minutes after it was first made available commercially, it was
readily obtainable on the black market and even today continues suspect in any number of unsolved kidnappings and
missing-persons cases. Rumor attributed its invention to the
Great Man. Schlaver read a statement denying his associate's
participation in the development of the chemical and asserting
how deeply the Inventor deplored the discovery of a product
so potentially pernicious. But rumor is not easily squelched,
and the whole affair left a bad taste.*

He is dozing in an armchair, three Furballs purring in his
lap. In the hall, the sound of his son's hoofs like a drumbeat on
the linoleum. His eyes flutter open, caught in the rift between
consciousness and the deeps. He stands. Gropes for his
glasses. Una lies asleep on the davenport, the snake coiled
round her like a meandering stream. He finds the tail. It
stiffens under his fingers, then goes limp. He heaves, fireman
and firehose: the coils spin to the carpet. "What's up?" Una
murmurs. He is unbuttoning her smock. The python lies on
the floor, dead weight, quietly digesting its bimonthly rabbit.
The Inventor climbs atop her, arching over her stiff as a
mounted butterfly. "I had a dream," he says.

from *The Life*

*It is now known that Una Moss was not the mother of the
Inventor's peculiarly deformed son. In fact, as Sissler and
Teebe have shown in* The Brewing Storm, *their perceptive
study of his last years, the Inventor and Miss Moss were never*

---

*A Cincinnati man, J. Leonard Whist, was prosecuted for possession of a controlled
substance, intent to do great bodily harm, and bigamy, when police found that he had
married four times, desiccated each of his wives, and reconstituted them as the whim
took him.

sexually intimate. The reason is simple: the Great Man was
impotent.

The son remains a problem.

The Inventor stands in the rain, surrounded by marble
monuments: angels, christs, bleeding hearts. Una and the boy
at his side. Their overcoats. Bowed heads. The smell of mold,
the open hole. The man in black reading from a book. It is
Schlaver's funeral. Cardiac arrest. The Inventor lingers after
the others have gone, the rain slanting down, and watches the
attendants as they slap the muddy earth on the coffin, scrape
it into the corners, tamp the reddish mound that rises above
the grass like bread in a pan. He stands there for a long while,
the eyes black, elbow tucked, fist under chin. Suddenly he
turns and hurries back to the limousine. Una and the boy are
there, the windows fogged. He snaps open his notebook and
begins scrawling equations across the page.

Three days later Schlaver is leaning back in an armchair at
the Westchester house, surrounded by reporters, lights, TV
cameras. He is in his bathrobe, looking much as he did before
death. The medical world is astounded. The press calls it a
hoax. The Inventor stands in the shadows, grinning.

from *The Life*

There were threatening phone calls. Windows were broken.
The house egged. The boy came home from school, blood on
the seat of his pants. His tail had been clipped. In the shower
room. It had been a pink tail, almost translucent, curled in
three tight coils like an angleworm, or the breath of a serpent.

The interviewer clears his throat, blows his nose in a
checked handkerchief, fiddles with the controls of the port-
able tape recorder. Una sits cross-legged on the carpet,
barefoot, a ring on each toe. She is lining up dominoes on the
coffee table, standing them on end in a winding file. The

Inventor is in his armchair; he is wearing a flannel shirt, sipping sherry. "And which of your myriad inventions," says the interviewer, "gives you the greatest personal satisfaction?" The Inventor looks down at the carpet, his fingers massaging the Furball in his lap. The wheels of the recorder whir, faint as the whine of a mosquito. "Those to come," he says. "Those that exist *ab ovo*, that represent possibility, moments of chemical reaction, epiphanies great and small. You must see of course that invention makes metaphor a reality, fixes—" but then he is interrupted by the clack of tumbling dominoes, regular as a second hand, beating like a train rushing over a bad spot in the rail. Una looks up, smiling, serene, her lips fat as things stung. The final domino totters. "Yes," says the Inventor. "Where were we?"

A Jewish star has been burned on his lawn. The Inventor is puzzled. He is not Jewish.

from *The Life*

The great work which had brooded so long on the Great Man's horizon came like Apocalypse. The world's ears stung. The work was met with cries of outrage, despair, resentment. Never, said his critics, have the hopes, the illusions, the dignity of mankind been so deflated in a single callous swipe. Fact, brutal undeniable naked fact, ate like a canker at all our hearts, they said. Who will reclothe our illusions? they asked. His friends hung their heads and feebly praised his candor. Others persisted in calling it a canard. It was no canard. How he had done it no one could begin to imagine. But there were the formulas for the experts to wonder at, and there, for all the world to see, were the slides. The color slides of God dead.

1) God, his great white beard, gauzy dressing gown, one arm frozen at half-mast. Supine. His mouth agape. Nebular backdrop.

2) *A top view. God stretching below the lens like a colossus, purple mountains' majesty, from sea to shining sea. Cloud foaming over his brow, hissing up from beneath his arms, legs, crotch.*

3) *The closeup. Eye sockets black, nostrils collapsed, the stained hairs of the beard, lips gone, naked hideous teeth.*

Night. Insects scraping their hind legs together, things stirring in the grass. Then the first cries, the flare of the torches. The earthquaking roar of the crowd. His neighbors are in the street, garden rakes and edgers poking over their massed heads, Yorkies and Schnauzers yanking them forward at the ends of leashes. Linked arm in arm, chanting "The Battle Hymn of the Republic," they come on, wrenching the great iron gates from their hinges, crushing through the beds of peonies, the banks of shrubbery, their faces savage and misaligned in the glare of the torches. Then the crash of the windows like a fever, the jeers of the women and children, husky brays of the men. And then the flames licking at the redwood planking, fluttering through the windows to chew at the drapes and carpets. The flash of Molotovs, the thunder of the little red cans of gasoline from a hundred lawn mowers. "Yaaaar!" howls the canaille at the first concussion. "Yaaaar!"

He is there. In the upper window. Una, Schlaver and the boy struggling to reach him from the fire escape. The flames, licking up twenty, thirty feet, framing the window like jagged teeth. The granite forehead, wisp of a beard, black eyes swimming behind the bottle lenses. Suddenly a cloud of smoke, dark as burning rubber, swells up and obscures the window. The crowd roars. When the smoke passes, the window is empty. Una's scream. Then the groan of the beams, the house collapsing in on itself with a rush of air, the neon cinders shooting high against the black and the stars, like the tails of a thousand Chinese rockets.

John Barleycorn Lives

There were three men came out of the West,
Their fortunes for to try.
And these three men made a solemn vow:
John Barleycorn must die.

            —"John Barleycorn" (traditional)

I WAS JUST LIFTING the glass to my lips when she stormed
through the swinging doors and slapped the drink out of
my hand. "Step back," she roared, "or suffer hellfire and
eternal damnation," and then she pulled a hatchet out from
under her skirts and started to splinter up Doge's new cher-
rywood bar. I ducked out of the way, ten-cent whisky darkening the crotch of my pants, and watched her light into the
glassware. It was like a typhoon in a distillery—nuggets of
glass raining down like hail, the sweet bouquet of that Scots
whisky and rum and rye going up in a mist till it teared your

eyes. Then Doge came charging out of the back room like a fresh-gelded bull, rage and bewilderment tugging at the corners of his mustache, just in time to watch her annihilate the big four-by-six mirror in the teakwood frame he'd had shipped up from New Orleans. BOOM! it went, shards of light washing out over the floor. Doge grabbed her arm as she raised the hatchet to put another cleft in the portrait of Vivian DeLorbe, but the madwoman swung round and caught him with a left hook. Down he went—and Vivian DeLorbe followed him.

The only other soul in the barroom was Cal Hoon, the artist. He was passed out at one of the tables, a bottle of whisky and a shot glass at his elbow. I was up against the back wall, ready to snatch up a chair and defend myself if necessary. The wild woman strode over to Cal's table and shattered the bottle with a hammering blow that jarred the derby from his head and left the hatchet quivering in the tabletop. And then the place was still. Cal raised his head from the table, slow as an old tortoise. His eyes were like smashed tomatoes and something dangled from the corner of his mouth. The mad woman stared down at him, hands on her hips. "Who hath woe? who hath sorrow? who hath babbling? who hath wounds without cause? who hath redness of eyes?" she demanded. Cal goggled up at her, stupefied. She pointed a finger at his nose and concluded: "He who tarries long at the wine." She must have been six feet tall. "Down on your knees!" she snarled, "and pray forgiveness of the Lord." Suddenly she kicked the chair out from under him and he toppled to the floor. A few taps from the toe of her boot persuaded him to clamber to his knees. Then she turned to me. I was Editor in Chief of *The Topeka Sun*, a freethinker, one of the intellectual lights of the town. But my knees cracked all the same as I went down and clasped my hands together. We sang "Art thou weary, art thou languid?", Cal's voice like a saw grinding through knotty pine, and then she was gone.

Two days later I was sitting at a table in the Copper Dollar Saloon over on Warsaw Street waiting for a steak and some fried eggs. John McGurk, my typesetter, was with me. It couldn't have been more than nine-thirty or ten in the morning. We'd been up all night getting out a special edition on McKinley's chances for a second term and we were drooping like thirsty violets. McGurk no sooner called for whisky and soda water than there she was, the madwoman, shoulders like a lumberjack's, black soutane from her chin to the floor. A file of women in black bonnets and skirts whispered in behind her. "Look here!" guffawed one of the bad characters at the bar. "It's recess time at the con-vent." His cronies cackled like jays. McGurk laughed out loud. I grinned, watchful and wary.

Her left eye was swollen closed, maroon and black; the other leered and goggled in a frightening, deranged way. She fixed the bad character with a look that would freeze a bowl of chili, and then she raised her arm and the women burst into song, their voices pitched high and fanatical, the rush of adrenalin and moral fervor swelling their bosoms and raking the rafters:

> Praise ye the Lord.
> Praise ye the Lord from the heavens:
> Praise ye Him in the heights.
> Praise ye Him, all ye angels:
> Praise ye Him, all His hosts.
> Praise ye Him, sun and moon.
> Praise ye Him, all ye stars of light.

We were defeated, instantly and utterly. The bad character hung his head, the barkeep wrung his bar rag, two of the cronies actually joined in the singing. McGurk cursed under his breath while I fought the impulse to harmonize, a childhood of choir rehearsals and gleaming organ pipes welling up in my eyes. Then she brandished the hatchet, waving it high

over her head like a Blackfoot brave, the other women following suit, drawing their weapons from the folds of their
gowns. They laid waste to the barroom, splinter by splinter,
howling hosannas all the while, and no one lifted a finger to
stop them.

I watched my beer foam out over the pitted counter, and
somewhere, from the depths of the building, I recognized the
odor of beefsteak burned to the bottom of an iron fry pan.

We decided to strike back. The ruins of the Copper Dollar
Saloon lay strewn about us: splinters and sawdust, the scalloped curls of broken glass, puddles of froth. I reached across
the table and grabbed hold of McGurk's wrist. "We'll do an
exposé, front page," I said, "and back it up with an editorial
on civil liberties." McGurk grinned like a weasel in a chicken
coop. I told him to get on the wire and dig up something on
Mrs. Mad that would take some of the teeth out of her bite.
Then I trundled off home to get some sleep.

An hour later he was knocking at my door. I threw on a robe
and opened up, and he burst into the parlor, his eyes shrunk
back and feverish. I offered him a chair and a brandy. He
waved them away. "Name's Carry Gloyd Nation," he said.
"Born in '46 in Kentucky. Married Charles Gloyd, M.D., in
'67—and get this—she left him after two months because he
was a rummy. She married Nation ten years later and he
divorced her just a few months back on the grounds of desertion."

"Desertion?"

"Yep. She's been running around tearing up saloons and
tobacco shops and Elks and Moose lodges all over the Mid-
west. Arrested in Fort Dodge for setting fire to a tobacco
shop, in Lawrence for tearing the dress off a woman in the
street because she was wearing a corset. Spent three days in

jail in St. Louis for assaulting the owner of a Chinese restaurant. She claims Chinese food is immoral."

I held up my palm. "All right. Fine. Go home and get some
sleep and then work this thing up for tomorrow's paper.
Especially the arrest record. We'll take some of the edge off
that hatchet, all right."

We ran the story next day. Two-inch headlines, front page.
On the inside, just under a thought-provoking piece on the
virtues of the motorcar as the waste-free vehicle of the future,
I ran a crisp editorial on First and Fourth Amendment
guarantees and the tyranny of the majority. It was a mistake.

By 8 A.M. there were two hundred women outside the
office singing "We Shall Overcome" and chaining themselves
to the railing. Banners waved over the throng, DEMON AL-
COHOL and JOHN BARLEYCORN MUST DIE, and one
grim woman held up a caricature of me with a bottle in my
hand and the sun sinking into its neck. The legend beneath it
read: THE TOPEKA SUN SETS.

None of my employees showed up for work—even McGurk
deserted me. At eight-fifteen his son Jimmy slipped into the
front office. He'd come to tell me his father was sick. Well so
was I. I bolted the door after him and dodged into the back
room to consult a bottle of Kentucky bourbon I kept on hand
for emergencies. I took a long swallow while snatches of song,
speechifying, cheers and shouts sifted in from the street.
Then there was a crash in the front office. I peered through
the doorway and saw that the window had been shattered—on
the floor beneath it lay the gleaming blade, tough oaken
handle of a hatchet.

Someone was pounding on the front door. I crept to the
window and peeped out. The crowd now filled the street.

Reverend Thorpe was there, a group of Mennonites in beards and black, another hundred women. I thought I saw McGurk's wife Lucy in the press, obscured by the slow helix of smoke that rose from a heap of still-folded newspapers. I wondered where the Sheriff was.

The door had now begun to heave on its hinges with each successive blow. It was at this point that I altered my line of perspective and saw that it was Mrs. Mad herself at the door, hammering away with the mallet head of her hatchet. "Open up!" she bellowed. "I demand a retraction of those Satan-serving lies! Open up I say!" On hands and knees, like an Indian fighter or a scout for Teddy Roosevelt, I made my way to the back room, took another pull at the bung and then ducked out the loading entrance. I tugged the hat down over my brow and headed for Doge's Place to regroup.

Doge had replaced the swinging doors with a three-inch-thick oak slab, which was kept bolted at all times. I tapped at the door and a metal flap opened at eye level. "It's me, Doge," I said, and the bolt shot back. Inside, two workmen were busy with hammer and saw, and Cal sat at a table with canvas, palette and a bottle of whisky, shakily reproducing the portrait of Vivian DeLorbe from the defaced original. Beside him, hanging his head like a skunked coonhound, was McGurk.

I stepped up to the improvised bar (a pair of sawhorses and a splintery plank) and threw down two quick whiskies. Then I sauntered over to join Cal and McGurk. McGurk muttered an apology for leaving me to face the music alone. "Forget it, John," I said.

"They got Lucy, you know," he said.

"I know."

Doge pulled up a chair and for a long moment we sat there silent, watching Cal trace the quivering perimeter of Vivian

DeLorbe's bust. Then Doge asked me if I was going to retract the story. I told him hell would freeze over first. McGurk pointed out that we'd be out of business in a week if I didn't. Doge cursed Mrs. Mad. McGurk cursed Temperance. We had a drink on it.

Cal laid down his brush and gave me a watery-eyed stare. "Know how you git yerself rid of 'er?"

"I'd give a hundred silver dollars to know that, friend," Doge said.

"Simple," Cal croaked, choking off to clear his throat and expectorate on the floor. "Git hold on that first hubband of hers—Doc Gloyd. Sight of him and she'll scare out of town like a horse with his ass-hairs afire."

The three of us came alive, hope springing eternal, et cetera, and we pressed him for details. Did he know Gloyd? Could he find him? Would Gloyd consent to it? Cal lifted the derby to smooth back his hair and then launched a windy narrative that jumped around like a palsied frog. Seems he'd been on a three-week drunk with "the Doc" in St. Louis's skid row six months earlier. The Doc had come into some money—a twenty-dollar gold piece—and the two of them had lain out in a field behind a distillery until they'd gone through it. "Fresh-corked bottles of the smoothest, fifty cent," said Cal, his eyes gone the color of butter. When he'd asked Gloyd about the twenty, Gloyd told him it was a token of gratitude from the thirsty citizens of Manhattan, Kansas. They'd paid his train fare and soaked him full of hooch to come out and rid the town of a plague.

"Mrs. Mad?" I said.

"You guessed it," said Cal, a rasping snicker working its way up his throat. "All she got to do is see him. It's liken to holdin a cross up front of a vampire."

Two hours later Cal and I were leaning back in the club car of the Atchison, Topeka and Santa Fe line, trying out their

sipping whisky, savoring a cigar, heading east. For St. Louis.
We were feeling pretty ripe by the time we stepped down
at the St. Louis station. I was a bit disoriented, what with the
railway yard alone half the size of Topeka proper, and what
with the rush of men in derby hats and short coats and women
with their backsides hefted up all out of proportion. Cal, on
the other hand, was right at home. He stooped to pluck up a
cigar butt and then swaggered through the crowd to where a
man, all tatters and ribs, sat propped against a bench like a
discarded parasol. The man sat on the pavement, his elbows
splayed on the bench behind him, head hanging as if his neck
had been broken. Cal plunked down beside him like a worn-
out drayhorse, oblivious to the suspicious-looking puddle the
fellow was sitting in. The man's eyelids drooped open as Cal
produced a bottle and handed it to him. The man drank, held
the bottle up for Cal. Cal drank, handed it back. They con-
ferred, sniggering, for five or ten minutes, then Cal rose with
a crack of knee and beckoned to me. "He's in town, all right,
the salty dog. Redfearns here seen him yestiddy." I glanced
down at Redfearns. He looked as if he hadn't seen anything in
a long while. "Is he sure?"
    "Down by the docks," Cal croaked, already whistling for a
hackney cab.

    We left our things—my things, Cal had nothing but the hat
on his head and a pair of suspenders—at Potter's Saloon, Beds
Five Cents, corner of Wharf St. and Albemarle Ave. Potter
sold us two bottles of local whisky for research purposes and
we strolled out to explore the underworld of the docks and
environs. Each time we passed a supine figure in the street
Cal stopped to make an identity check, and if expedient, to
revive it with a slug or two of Potter's poison. Then followed a
period of bottle passing and sniggering colloquy that twinned
the Redfearns encounter as if they'd rehearsed it.

After a while I found myself heaving down beside Cal and these reeking winesoaks, the sun building a campfire under my hat, trousers soiled, taking my turn when the bottle was passed. There I sat, Editor in Chief of *The Topeka Sun*, a freethinker and one of the intellectual lights of the town, on the blackened cobblestones of St. Louis's most disreputable streets, my judgment and balance eroded, vision going, while lazy bluebottles floated between the sweat-beaded tip of my nose and the mounds of horseshit that lay round us like a series of primitive sculptures. All in the cause of humanity.

As the day wore on I began to lose touch with my surroundings. I rose when Cal touched my arm, collapsed like a rump-shot dog when he stopped to interrogate another souse. We walked, talked and drank endlessly. I remember a warehouse full of straw boaters and whalebone corsets, a bowl of chili and a cup of black coffee in a walk-up kitchen, a succession of filthy quays, garbage bins, toothless faces and runny eyes. But no Gloyd. When the sun finally lurched into the hills, Cal took me by the elbow and steered us back to Potter's.

I was discouraged, disheartened, and thanks to Potter's home brew, nearly disemboweled. After puking against the side of a carriage and down the front of my shirt, there was only one thing I wanted from life: a bed. Potter (the only thing I remember about him is that he had the most flaccid, pendulous jowls I'd ever seen on man or beast—they looked like nothing so much as buttocks grafted onto his face) led me up the stairs to the dormitory and gave me a gentle shove into the darkened room. "Number Nine," he said. When my eyes became accustomed to the light I saw that the ranks of wooden bedsteads were painted with white numbers. I started down the row, reeling and reeking, fighting for balance, until I drew up to Number Nine. As I clutched at the bedpost with my left hand and fought to unbutton my shirt with my right, I became aware of a form beneath the horse-hair blanket spread across my bunk. Someone was in my bed. This was too much. I began to shake him. "Hey, wake up there, pardner. That's my bunk you got there. Hey." It was then that I lost my footing and tumbled atop him.

He came alive like a whorehouse fire, screeching and writhing. "Buggery!" he shrieked. "Murder and sodomy!" The other occupants of the dormitory, jolted awake, began spitting threats and epithets into the darkness. I tried to extract myself but the madman had my head in a vise-grip. His voice was high-pitched and spasmodic, a sow scenting the butcher's block. "Pederasty!" he bawled.

Suddenly the room blazed with light. It was Potter, wagging his inhuman jowls, a lantern in his hand. Cal stood at his elbow, squinting into the glare. I turned my head. The man who had hold of me was hoary as a goat, yellow-toothed, his eyes like the eggs of some aquatic insect. "Doc!" shouted Cal.

The madman loosened his grip. "Cal?" he said.

McGurk met us at the Topeka station and gave us the lay of the land. A group of them—women in black bonnets, teetotalers and Holy Rollers—were still picketing the office, and in the absence of *The Sun* had begun an alternative press in the basement of the Baptist church. McGurk showed me a broadside they'd printed. It described me as "a crapulous anarchist," "a human viper," and "a lackey of the immoral and illicit business enterprises which prey on the emotionally feeble for the purpose of fiduciary gain." But a syntactical lashing wasn't the worst of it. Mrs. Mad had bought off the Sheriff and she and her vigilantes were scouring the town in the name of Jesus Christ, sobriety and abstinence from tobacco, fraternity and Texicano food. She'd evacuated the Moose Lodge and Charlie Trumbull's Tobacco Emporium, and then her disciples had boarded up the doors. And she'd closed down Pedro

Páramo's eatery because he served fresh-pounded tortillas and refried beans with an order of eggs. It was high time for a showdown.

We threw open the massive oaken door at Doge's Place, took the boards down from the new plate-glass windows, lit the oil lamps, and hired a one-legged banjo strummer from Arkansas to cook us up some knee-slapping music. Before Cal had finished tracing the big winged *D* for DOGE'S PLACE on the front window, the saloon was shoulder-deep in drinking men, including a healthy salting of bad characters. That banjo rang and thrilled through the streets like the sweet song of the Sirens. Somebody even fired off a big horse pistol once or twice.

Our secret weapon sat at the bar. His fee was fifty dollars and all he could drink. Doge had donated a bottle of his finest, and I took up a collection for the rest, beginning with a greenback ten out of my own pocket. Gloyd was pretty far gone. He stared into his empty shot glass, mooing her name over and over like a heifer coming into heat. "Carry. Ohhh, Carry."

Doge refilled his glass.

It took her half an hour. On the nose. Up the street she came, grim and foreboding, her jackals and henchwomen in tow. I lounged against the doorframe, picking my teeth. The banjo rang in my ears. I could see their heads thrown back as they shrieked out the lyrics of some spiritual or other, and I felt the tremor as their glossy black boots descended on the pavement in unison, tramp, tramp, tramp. Up the street, arms locked, teeth flashing, uvulas aquiver. "He is my refuge and my fortress!" they howled. Tramp, tramp, tramp. She led them up the porch, shoved me aside, and bulled her way in.

Suddenly the place fell silent. The banjo choked off, yahoos and yip-hays were swallowed, chatter died. She raised her arm and the chorus swept up the scale to finish on a raging high C, pious and combative. Then she went into her act, snorting and stamping round the room till her wire-rimmed spectacles began to mist up with emotion. "Awake, ye drunkards, and weep!" she roared. "Howl, all ye drinkers of wine, for strong drink shall be bitter to them that drink it." She was towering, swollen, red-faced, awesome as a twister roaring up out of the southwest. We were stunned silent—Cal, Doge, McGurk, Pedro—all of us. But then, from the rear of the crowd, all the long way down the far end of the bar, came the low moan of ungulate distress. "Carrrrry, ohhhh baby, what have I done to you?"

The look on her face at that moment could have constituted a criminal act in itself. She was hideous. There was a scuffle of chairs and feet as we cleared out of her way, every man for himself. Doge ducked down behind the bar, Cal and McGurk sought refuge back of an overturned table, the bad characters made themselves scarce, and suddenly there were just the two of them—Mrs. Mad and Gloyd—staring into each other's eyes across the vacant expanse of the barroom. Gloyd got down off the bar stool and started toward her, his gait shuffling and unsteady, his arms spread in a vague empty embrace. Suddenly the hatchet appeared in her hand, legerdemain, her knuckles clenched white round the handle. She was breathing like a locomotive, he was calm as comatose. She started toward him.

When they got within two yards of one another they stopped. Gloyd tottered, swaying on his feet, a lock of yellowed hair catching in his eye socket. "Carry," he said, his voice rough and gutteral. "Honey, peachblossom, come back to me, come back to your old Doc." And then he winked at her.

She flushed red, but then got hold of herself and came back at him with the Big Book: "At the last it biteth like a serpent, and stingeth like an adder."

He looked deep into her eyes, randy as an old coyote. "I am
like a drunken man, and like a man whom wine hath overcome." He was grinning. He raised his arms to embrace her
and suddenly she lashed out at him with the hatchet, the arc
and the savage swish of it as it sliced the air, missing him by a
clean two feet or more. "Carry," he said, his voice sad and
admonishing. "Let bygones be bygones honey and come on
back to your old Doc." Her arm fell, the hatchet dropped to
the floor. She hung her head. And then, just a whisper at first,
he began crooning in a rusty old voice, soft and sad, quavering
like a broken heart:

> The huntsman he can't hunt the fox,
> Nor so loudly to blow his horn,
> And the tinker he can't mend kettle nor pot,
> Without a little barleycorn.

When he finished we stood there silent—the women in black,
the bad characters, Doge, Cal, McGurk and me—as though
we'd just watched the big brocaded curtain fall across the
stage of Tyler's Playhouse in Kansas City. And then suddenly
she fell to her knees sobbing—wailing and clucking in the
back of her throat till I couldn't tell if it was laughing or
crying. Her sobs, like her fulminations, were thunderous—
they filled the room, shook the rafters. I began to feel embarrassed. But the Doc, he just stood over her, hands on his hips,
grinning, until one of the women—it was Lucy McGurk—
helped her from the room.

The faces of her retinue were pale as death against their
black bonnets and choirboy collars. No longer the core of a
moral cyclone, they were just townswomen, teetotalers and
pansies. We jeered like the bad characters we were, and they
turned tail and ran.

A month later a wagon rumbled up Warsaw Street from the station with Doge's new mahogany bar counter in back. McGurk and I took the afternoon off to sit in the cool dusk of Doge's Place and watch Doge and Cal nail it down and put the first coat of wax on it. The new Vivian DeLorbe, a bit rippled, but right in the right spots, hung proudly, and a sort of mosaic mirror—made up of pieces salvaged from the original and set in plaster—cast its submarine reflections round the room. We had a couple of whiskies, and then Doge mentioned he'd heard Mrs. Mad was back at it again, parching all the good citizens down in Wichita. Cal and I laughed, but poor John didn't take it so well, seeing that Lucy had left him to go off with her and join the movement.

Cal shook his head. "These women," he said. "There's no stoppin 'em. Next thing you know they'll be wantin the vote."

Drowning

IN THIS STORY, someone will drown. Yet there will be no apparent reason for this drowning—it will not for example be attributable to suicide, murder, divine retribution—nor even such arcana as current and undertow. It will instead be like so many events of the future: inexplicable, incomprehensible. Nonetheless, it will occur.

There is a girl alone on the beach, a mere inkspot in the white: nothing really, when compared with the massive dunes that loom behind her and the sea, dark and implacable, which stretches before her to Europe and Africa. She is lying there on her back, eyes closed, her body loose, toes pointing straight out to the water. Her skin glistens with oil, tanned deep as a ripe pear. And she wears a white bikini: two strips of cloth as dazzlingly white in this sun as the sand itself. She is after an effect, a contrast.

Now she sits up, the taut line of her abdomen bunching in soft creases, and glances slyly around. No one in sight up and down the beach, for miles perhaps—the only sign of life the gull beating overhead, muttering in its prehistoric voice. Her hands reach behind for the strings to the bikini halter—the elbows strain out in sharp triangles and her back arches, throwing her chest forward. She feels a quick pulse of excitement as her breasts fall free and the sea breeze tickles against them. She's brown here too—a shade lighter than her shoulders and abdomen, but still tanned deeply.

She falls back on her elbows, face to the sun, the hair soft down her back and into the sand. The gull is gone now, and the only sounds are the hiss of the foam and the plangent thunder of the breakers smoothing rock a hundred yards out. She steals another look round—a good long one, over her shoulders and up to the peaks of the dunes. No one. "Why not?" she thinks. "Why not?" And her thumbs ease into the elastic band that girds her hips, working it down, kicking her legs free of it, stretching and spreading herself to the sun. But here she is white, ridiculously white, white as the bikini, white as the breakers.

Then she lets her head fall back again, closes her eyes, points her toes. But she can't hold it for long—she feels something, a racing inside that makes her breath quick—and she raises her head to look long down her body: the breasts high on her chest, the sharp declivity of the ribcage, the smooth abdomen, the tightly wound hairs. The sun on her body is languid, warm: a massage. At her side: the tanning oil, cooking in the sun. She uncaps the plastic bottle, squeezes, feels the hot spurt of it across her chest. Then her palms are smoothing over the skin in a slow circular motion and she remembers how they'd all studied her with their hot faces while she sat above them, a Greek statue, staring out the window. From their expressions she could tell it wasn't like

sketching a professional model—they'd seen her around campus so many times and so many times had looked up her skirt
and down her blouse, undressing her with their eyes. And
then suddenly, a shock: there she was. She thinks of those
faces, those nervous hands, hairy wrists. And laughs, laughs
while her fingers move in the ripening sun—smoothly, thrill-
ingly—over her body.

Five hundred yards down the beach, the man ends his hike
and approaches the water's edge. He kicks about in the sand
while the soft foaming fringe shoots over his toes, up to his
ankles and on past to retrace a broad ellipse in the sand behind him. He seems satisfied with the spot. Everything pleas-
antly symmetrical: the dark line of the high tide, the rounded
peaks of the dunes, the fanned circular waves riding in on an
infinity of waves, each identical to the first. Yes, he is
satisfied, and like any other bather he wades in, the water
rising gradually up his thin pale legs. But he is an anomaly
here—his skin shows no trace of a tan—not the smallest
freckle. Is this then his first day on the beach? He looks
unhealthy and thin, too white in this flashing sun.

He wades deeper and the water washes level with his groin,
the roll of the waves gently floating his genitals. The sensation, after the first shock, is cool and smooth, like the breath
of an air conditioner. Is he aware, as he turns his head to look
down the beach, that the girl, drowsing now despite herself,
is naked and alone—defenseless even? I think not. There is
certainly something down there in the distance, obscured by
the glare and the heat haze. Something dark, a stain in the
whiteness. But really, it's none of his concern. The waves lap
at his underarms, splash up into his beard—and then he dives
smooth into the next tall one, spearing through like a dolphin.
He kicks powerfully and speeds through the incoming peaks
until he is a considerable distance from shore. From his per-

formance in the water, it is apparent that this is his element, that the paleness he displayed on the beach has no bearing here. Far from shore, his head is a buoy, tentatively riding up on the distant blinding whitecaps.

She strolled into the classroom in a short white smock. The hem of the smock defined a sharp line across the rise of her buttocks. It lifted and fell with each deliberate step. The art students, the ones who'd absently sketched a dozen models before her, now practically leaped from their chairs. She recognized nearly all of them from around campus, had ignored their slick hungry looks on countless occasions. She knew the girls too—they colored a bit when she entered, shifted in their seats from buttock to buttock. A few glared. But she just strolled, calmly, confidently, her chest thrust forward, just strolled right to the center of the room, yawned a brief yawn and then unbuttoned the smock, and let it fall to the floor.

In the broad expanse of the dunes a pair of wide feet wanders, kicking channels in the hot sand, becoming buried and unburied alternately as they are lifted from one spot to the next. Bobbing along, just ahead of the shuffling feet, is a circular shadow. Its unwitting creator is an obese young man, dressed in T-shirt and bathing trunks—the baggy boxer type with a broad red stripe on each side. Clenched in his left hand is a towel. Every few moments the towel rises to his face and flaps about in an effort to mop up the perspiration. Brackish creeks and streams and rivulets wash over the globe of his torso and down his legs to dot the sand. He apparently has come a good distance, but why through the harsh dunes? If, as I suspect, he is looking for a secluded stretch of sea for bathing, why doesn't he walk along the beach, where temperatures are cooler and footing easier?

He approaches the crest of the final dune blocking his way

to the beach, the sea breeze stiff in his nostrils and cool against his face. Feet splayed, his legs attack the slope—the band of ocean visible over the lip of the dune grows wider, opening like an eye, with each plodding step upward. Finally, with a great wet heave of breath, he reaches the summit. Ah! The wind in his hair, the sea, the lone gull coasting overhead, solitude! But no, there below him is . . . a female! Nude and asleep! He starts back, vanishes. And then, on his belly in the sand, takes a lingering look. Her breasts, flattened with gravity, nipples pointing heavenward, her black-haired pubes! Beneath him, another part of the body, just a small appendage, adds itself to the general tumescence.

One hour. They had one hour to leer to their hearts' content—she wasn't even watching—her gaze was fixed on the bell tower out the window and across the campus. They were crowding in, faces blank, scholars. Scholars operating under the premise that she was just a specimen, headless and mindless, a physique, a painted beetle fixed beneath a microscope.

She knew better.

Tomorrow they wouldn't dare approach her, yet they'd stare even harder, straining to see up her skirt and down her blouse, grinning like jackals. They'd leer and joke as if she were some kind of freak. And she would be distant, haughty. They'd had their hour, and that was that. The closest any of them would ever come to her. In bed in the dark they would fitfully strain to summon her image, but like all mental pictures it would come in flashes, a film out of frame. She knew all this, and as she posed that day the faintest trace of a smile rounded her lips: inscrutably.

All his life he'd been forced to contend with sniggers, grinning faces, pointed fingers. People looked on him as a bad joke—a caricature of themselves, some sort of cosmic admonition to keep their noses clean. They laughed to cover their horror, laughed, imagining their own eyes pinched behind those sagging cheeks and chins. And often as not they resorted to violent pranks. He had for instance been obliged to discontinue regular attendance at the high school when he found he couldn't walk the halls without having his head slapped from behind by some invisible hand or having the books pushed from his arms to spray beneath hundreds of trampling feet. On one occasion eight or nine lean toughs had lined the wall outside his chemistry class, and when he emerged had enthusiastically decorated his physiognomy with lemon chiffon, coconut custard and Boston cream. After that, his parents decided that perhaps home tutoring would be more viable.

Since the time of these experiences he had very rarely entertained the company of others, had very rarely in fact left his parents' home. In the winter it was the apartment, in the summer the beach house. His social phobia was so overwhelming that he refused to show himself in public under any circumstance, not even in so trivial a role as picking up half a pound of pastrami at the delicatessen around the corner or taking the wash to the laundromat. He was a hermit, a monk, a solipsist. In the summer he would walk for miles through the dunes so he could swim alone without fear of exposing himself to ridicule, the preponderance of his flesh displayed in a swimsuit.

The upshot of all this is that he had, at the time of this story, reached the age of twenty-one years without ever having been laid. He had never been on a date, had never brushed a cheek against his own, had never squeezed a sweating palm or tit.

He stands, decides to have a closer look. But what if she should wake? The thought attenuates his resolve and he freezes there at the dune's crest, staring, obsessed. Just like in the nudist magazines. Masturbatory fantasies recur, charge through his head like rams—this is just the situation he had always pictured alone in his room, pulling furiously at his pud.

Soon he becomes increasingly conscious of the heat and removes his T-shirt, dropping it carelessly beside him, his attention fixed on the browned peaks below. He starts stealthily down the slope: a sly beast stalking its prey. But in a moment he's sliding down out of control, a truckload of sand following him. The seat of his trunks fills with it. At the base of the dune he recovers himself, jumps up, afraid to breathe, his rear abraded and an uncomfortable projection straining against the zipper of his trunks. The trunks begin to annoy him: he removes them.

A course of action is not entirely clear to him, but he moves closer anyhow, now as naked as she. The breasts swell gently with her sleep, the legs stir, the tongue peeps out to moisten her lips. And then suddenly the feathery warmth of the sun becomes a hot oppressive burden and she wakes to a huge childish face in her own and an insistent poking between her thighs. She shrieks, pushes wildly at that fat face. But she's pinned beneath a truck, she's been involved in an accident, that's it, a mountain has fallen and she's trapped beneath it. (Sure he's embarrassed but how can he stop now, the blood swelling up in him as it is?)

Cheeks clawed and gashed, eardrums aching, sweating like a frosted goblet, he drives relentlessly on. He inserts a massive fist in her mouth to quiet the wailing, and inadvertently, as he stiffens toward his moment of truth, he shoves increasingly harder, her head smoothing a depression in the sand—a basin for the blood that seeps from her mashed lips, loosened teeth. She gasps, croaks for air. Below, the white triangle is smothered beneath a sea of convulsively heaving flesh, and furtively, deep within, it too begins to bleed.

"Hey!" yell the fishermen. (They'd been poking around up the shore, drinking beer from a cooler, hunting in a half-assed way for stripers or porgies or blues.) "Hey!" And then they begin running toward what looks like a giant sea turtle digging frantically to bury its eggs.

His head rears up in surprise. With a grunt he disengages himself from her body and his fist from her mouth. An enamel cap, embedded between the second and third knuckles of his left hand, comes with it. He stands there for a blind moment, naked, dripping blood, caught in the act of committing an atrocity. He feels shame, mortification, guilt, remorse, self-denigration—and a rabid animal impulse to escape at any cost. He lumbers in a panic toward the sea, his only possible refuge. The fishermen reach the girl just as he is parting the waves, a colossal preterrestrial creature more at home in the sea than on land. "Hey!" the fishermen shout. But he is gone, paddling furiously, smashing the waves like an icebreaker. Deeper and deeper, farther and farther from his pursuers and his own fat life.

The fishermen are standing in the surf, their shoes and pants wet. They bellow a few drunken imprecations but he is already too distant to care. He drifts off on the waves, a great lump of sperm seeking to impregnate the sea. The fishermen turn back to the whimpering girl. One gently cups his hand under her chin while the other removes his trousers and sets to her.

Far out to sea, far beyond the churning fat boy and the rapacious fishermen, that strange pale creature floats, peacefully drowsing. His beard and long hair fan out in the water, become masses of seaweed. A chance wave, peaking higher than the others, rolls over him and he swallows a quantity of water. The next buries him. He has had no warning, no chance to cry for help, no hope that help would be available.

Quite simply then, he drowns. A random event, one that I imagine, considering the world as a whole, is quite common.

The fat boy creeps home naked through the dark dunes, miles from where he had first encountered the girl. His feet and lower legs are lacerated from the stiff dune grass which bites into each blind step. In all, he feels a vague sense of shame, but also a certain exhilaration. After all, he's finally made the first palpable step in overcoming his social inadequacy.

The fishermen are at home, watching color TV. They feel a deep and abiding sense of accomplishment, of fulfillment— though they returned home this afternoon with an empty porgy basket.

The girl sleeps a heavy drugged sleep, enfolded in the astringently white hospital sheets. Her tan contrasts nicely with them. The breath passes gently through her parted lips, lips battered and brown with dried blood. A gray-haired man (her father?) sits beside her, patting her sleeping hand.

The thin man, the pale one, is jerked spasmodically by the underwater currents, tangled in a bed of weed. The crabs have long since discovered him and are rattling their ancient horny shells about his flesh, delighted with the unexpected treat. The tide is washing in, and the drowned man with it. Eventually, I suspect, what is left of him will come to rest on the beach, a few yards away from a curious red-brown stain in the bleached sand. The half-cleaned skeletons and carapaces of other strange creatures lie there too, waiting for the morning's gulls.

For a complete list of books available from Penguin in the United States, write to Dept. DG, Penguin Books, 299 Murray Hill Parkway, East Rutherford, New Jersey 07073.

For a complete list of books available from Penguin in Canada, write to Penguin Books Canada Limited, 2801 John Street, Markham, Ontario L3R 1B4.